A Corporation
of
Angels

James H. Barrett Jr.

abbott press

Abbott Press books may be ordered through booksellers or by contacting:

Abbott Press
1663 Liberty Drive
Bloomington, IN 47403
www.abbottpress.com
Phone: 1 (866) 697-5310

ISBN: 978-1-4582-1998-5 (sc)
ISBN: 978-1-4582-1999-2 (hc)
ISBN: 978-1-4582-2000-4 (e)

Library of Congress Control Number: 2016902533

Print information available on the last page.

Abbott Press rev. date: 02/23/2016

ACKNOWLEDGEMENTS

First and foremost, I want to thank God for the creativity and many blessings that have been bestowed on mine and my wife's lives.

I would like to thank my friend Paul Mulach and his magic pencil, which turned a picture into an awesome cover sketch for this book.

I would like to thank my friend Tony Robenalt, for his expertise in grammar, punctuation and much appreciated recommendations regarding this story.

I would like to thank my wife, Belva, for her ideas, support and always having confidence in me.

I dedicate this book
to all of the people
who have touched my
life in some way, both
here now and already
gone from this world.

INTRODUCTION

It was the start of a typical workday in Pittsburgh, Pennsylvania. The sunrise was beginning to poke through the buildings downtown. It was a cool spring morning; people were getting off buses and scurrying separate ways to their workplaces. Horns were echoing from impatient drivers. Some people were delaying the inevitable, taking their time as they were in no hurry to start the workday. A few people stood outside of the Dunkin Donuts sipping a morning coffee, across from the Steel Building located at 600 Grant Street, claimed as the tallest building in Pittsburgh, standing at sixty-four stories high and housing numerous companies.

Directly behind the Steel Building was a building which very few people knew about. The sign on the outside of the building read C.O.A. Inc. Under the company name was the address, One His Way. The building was in the shape of a cross. The composition was mainly glass with gold and brilliant colored stone that shone like a rainbow from the sunlight. The building had a beautiful view of the city, especially at the top, since it was one hundred stories high. I know you are thinking, Wait a minute, I thought the Steel Building was the highest building in Pittsburgh? Hold that thought. We will come back to it. Unlike the Steel Building, C.O.A. Inc. had only one employer occupying the structure, and everyone loved their job.

The employees at C.O.A. looked like anyone else bustling through the city. Some were dressed in a suit or casual dress, while others were fully clad as maintenance workers or in security uniforms. There was nothing out of the ordinary that would call attention to them. The offices looked like any other office, complete with cubicles. Each cube had its own desk, chair, phone, computer, along with other normal office equipment. There was a conference room on each floor, with an auditorium near the top of the building that was used for all employee meetings. The ninety-eighth floor was a command center that was used to communicate with workers in the field. C.O.A. was a twenty-four hour operation, contrasting most other offices.

Working at C.O.A. would be considered more of a hands-on atmosphere. It involved more than sitting in an office, with your face buried in a computer. Much of the work took place on the streets among people. One day you could be in the office, collecting information on the computer, and then the very same evening you would be in New York City, keeping an eye on a client. One thing was for sure, it was never boring.

At eight o'clock every morning there was a meeting held in the conference rooms on each floor to discuss the business of the day. Everyone was expected to be at the meeting unless they were working in the field at that time. C.O.A. had team leaders for specific projects at different times, but none permanently. All employees were colleagues, except for the C.E.O., who oversaw the whole operation. Duties were handed out daily to the staff. Each floor in the building made up a group. Depending on the size the job, it could encompass the whole set or only a few of the group. *They always worked in pairs of two or more, never alone.* All C.O.A. employees carried a smart phone, so they could keep in constant contact with their colleagues while in the field.

It was 7:50 a.m. and the employees had started trickling into their assigned conference rooms for the morning update. As the workers filed into the room, they pulled up a seat and chatted quietly while waiting for the project leader to take his or her place at the podium situated in the front of the room. Promptly at 8:00 a.m. the project leaders approached the podium on ninety-eight of the one hundred floors in the building. The auditorium on the ninety-ninth floor shared a small section of office space with A.R., which we will get to shortly. It was the widest part of the building and gave it the look of a cross. The one hundredth floor was reserved as the Penthouse office for the C.E.O.

On the second floor, the team leader was a balding man who looked to be in his early forties. He wore a blue bow tie with a white shirt and navy colored pants and sport coat. He tapped the microphone to get everyone's attention.

"Good morning," he announced.

"Good morning," everyone responded cheerfully.

"I am Michael, for those who don't know me, I will be your project leader this morning. To my right, is my partner, Mary." He motioned to the woman sitting beside him. She nodded to the crowd and smiled. She was dressed accordingly, matching Michael's attire.

"Now that introductions have been made, let's get to the business of the day. We have a small problem on the Allegheny River, near the 16th Street Bridge. We will need four of you to leave now to handle the situation."

Two sets of partners volunteered, took a slip of paper from Michael and left the meeting hurriedly.

"There is a mechanical problem at the convention center, which will require eight additional workers." Michael lifted his head to see four sets of partners dressed in maintenance uniforms walking toward the podium. He handed them paperwork, then thanked them as they headed to the exit. Michael continued to hand out assignments that called for work around the city for the day, most of which needed two or four workers to complete the task. When he had finished, he asked the remaining employees to return to their offices to resume data collection. Depending on the day's events, they could be needed for field work at a later time. Michael reminded everyone to call 811 if something urgent came up. The call would go directly to his phone. Everyone adjourned from the meeting and returned to their cubes.

CHAPTER 1

By now, it is clear that you probably have many unanswered questions. Let's try to fill you in. C.O.A. stands for Corporation of Angels. The C.E.O., of course, is God. The address, 1 His Way, needs no further explanation. What else would it be? *Who are the employees,* you are wondering? Well, as a matter of fact, they are angels...

The angels were allowed to pick their own names at C.O.A. Many of them liked to pick the well-known angel names. Because of that, the name could only be used once in each department. Sometimes the angels had more than one assignment. That was one reason each angel had a partner. Every assignment was important and deserved the correct amount of attention. Another reason was that two heads were better than one. No mistakes were to be made. Lastly, it was for teamwork. Working together and getting along was what it was all about. Loving each other and taking care of everyone was the purpose. There were no favorites at C.O.A. That was why project leaders were picked daily for the most part, unless the project needed more attention than one day to fulfill. Some angels volunteered for long-term missions. Many of these assignments required them to spend more time involved in changing the attitudes of people, or groups of people.

Gabriel and his partner Sarah were two of the angels on a special mission. Each city had at least one or more sets of angels, who were on special assignment. Some of the bigger cities such as Los Angeles or New York could have up to ten groups of angels assigned. The special detail that Gabriel, Sarah and the others were currently assigned to was called Project Lost Faith. It had come to everyone's attention that many people were losing faith in God, particularly in America. It was the angels' duty to do what they could to turn that around. At the moment, it had been a high priority mission, with all eyes watching, especially the C.E.O. of C.O.A.

Gabriel liked to wear bowling shirts, khaki pants and a Kangol hat turned backward. He wore longer hair than most of the other angels. It was shoulder length, blond and curly, and he looked to be in his early thirties. His partner Sarah, appeared to be in her late twenties to early thirties as well. She had short black hair and was dressed casually too. They looked like a typical Pittsburgh yuppie couple. That was the target audience that C.O.A. was trying to focus on. These younger people were moving into neighborhoods, where they would buy their first house and begin to raise a family of their own. At the moment, Gabriel and Sarah rented a house on the east side of Pittsburgh, where there was concern regarding non-believers in the area. The two of them were to blend in and help to adjust the thinking of some of their neighbors. They had to do this without revealing their true identity, which took some ingenuity. When their job was done, they would move to a new neighborhood and start over. Gabriel and Sarah had been working on this mission for the past two weeks, among the *walking souls*. That was how the angels referred to human beings.

When the angels mingled with people, they looked just like any other walking soul. They had no wings or halos around their heads. That way, they blended in with everyone else. Very young children and mentally challenged walking souls saw the angels in their true state. They were clothed in brilliant white gowns and barefoot, with two sets of glorious wings. They also had an amazing glow about them. Once children were old enough to talk, they usually no longer saw the angels as they truly were. Everyone has seen a baby giggling for no reason. It is quite possible that the appearance of a magnificent angel has caught their attention. A mentally challenged person has seen angels all of his or her life, and their guardian angel has always been a constant companion. He or she became their best friend and it seemed quite normal for them. An angel could also choose to be invisible on certain occasions as well. One circumstance would be when an angel had to act in an extremely quick amount of time to defuse a situation. For example, one might need to stop a car accident in a hurry. There would be no time to waste, and if someone suddenly appeared in your car out of nowhere, it would not be a good scenario. Think about the situation for a second. At the very least, the walking soul could soil their pants. For that reason, the angel would take control of the car without the walking soul knowing what had happened.

Back at C.O.A., the angels had been hard at work. Many of them were on their computers, receiving information for assignments already in progress, as well as upcoming assignments. All information came from the mainframe on the one hundredth floor, which was supplied by the C.E.O. Most days were frantic. Everything had to be concise, thorough, and flawless, but the angels were used to the demands of their positions. Other than children, mentally challenged, or very sick individuals, a walking soul could not see the C.O.A. building either, just like they couldn't see the angels in their true state, as previously mentioned. That was why the Steel Building was the highest building in Pittsburgh, at least as far as walking souls knew. If a walking soul ventured around the back of the Steel Building, they would see no evidence of C.O.A., just a 7-Eleven and a hotel in their view. It was also the most spectacular building in the world, with its shining gold, lined with rubies, emeralds and diamonds. The windows were staggered with amazing stained-glass and unblemished clear windows, which had the most stunning view of the city and its three rivers. On a clear day from the ninety-ninth floor, you could see for miles around the city. The view from Mt. Washington would even take a back seat.

Michael and Mary received a call from the two teams of angels that were dispatched to the river during the morning meeting. The situation had been defused. It seemed that there was a fully loaded barge moving dangerously close to one of the uprights on the Sixteenth Street Bridge. The captain had been preoccupied with problems at home and was not concentrating on his job. One team turned the captain's attention to the danger by knocking a coffee cup onto the floor. The angels were in an invisible mode at that time. When the captain looked up, he saw the proximity of the bridge beam, steered the barge away, and the accident was diverted. The other team eased the captain's mind from the tension regarding his family. His son had been acting up in school, but two more angels were set in place to join his class and then befriend him to get him back on track. A barge smashing into the Sixteenth Street Bridge at 8:30 a.m. would be catastrophic. The bridge was full of commuters making their way into the city at that time of morning.

The four teams that had been sent to the convention center were still on the job. There was a problem with the foundation on the property. A car convention was due in town the following morning, and there would be a lot of weight in the building. Cracks had been found in the building's foundation and needed to be repaired to fend off multiple casualties. The maintenance crew of the building hadn't seen the problems, and there was not enough time for them to fix it. The angels were on their own for the discrete safeguarding effort. They assured Michael that they would be finished before long.

In addition to repairing the cracks in the foundation, the teams had to install additional supports at the base of the building, to shore it up.

It was a busy day in the office. In the Accounting Department, angels kept track of the finances of all walking souls in the area. Given the recession, many people were juggling bills and trying to make ends meet. The angels would discretely help them to avoid making bad decisions. Desperation could lead them into big trouble. Money troubles could sometimes cause people to con, steal or even murder one another. One of the duties of an angel in accounting was to help people not to get to that point. It could be as simple as whispering a helpful idea in one's ear, regarding a bad investment decision. It could involve a visit from a family member or friend who could offer a gift or loan to help them out. Sometimes it could involve a promotion at work or even a career change.

There was also a Supply Chain and Inventory Department at C.O.A. The angels in that department supplied cash and equipment needed for the employees while they were among the walking souls. The angels filled out requisition forms, like any other corporation. At the end of an assignment, a Return Authorization form, or R.A. for short, was filled out. Then the material was inspected and restored in place. There was a thirty story warehouse in the Strip District, which housed everything you could imagine. Cars, motorcycles, boats, and anything else you might envision was stored there. If a walking soul could have seen it, one might have thought they were standing in Jay Leno's garage!

There was also a Marketing Department. It was an essential component of the corporation. As you might have already figured out, their job was to keep walking souls informed about God. Not only on Sunday in church, but in everyday life. He wanted to be part of your life in places like Facebook, Twitter and other social media. Things changed constantly, and the marketing team needed to stay abreast of the changing culture. Gabriel and Sarah were well respected employees of the marketing team.

The majority of the workforce were in the Customer Relations Department. These were the worker bees. They were usually sent out on multiple assignments per day. It could be as simple as smiling at someone having a bad day. It could also be an extreme case, which called for a stranger to console a walking soul in great despair. Sometimes, all people needed was someone to talk to. Angels were good listeners. How could they not be? Look who they worked for.

CHAPTER 2

Jeremiah and Jonah were partners who worked in Customer Relations. Jonah was transferred from the west coast office a few years back when he partnered up with Jeremiah. While in their walking soul persona, they couldn't be more conspicuous. Jeremiah was tall and sleek with well-groomed short brown hair. He also liked to wear a suit. He would put you in mind of Liam Neeson. Jonah, on the other hand, was short and pudgy with a shaved head and a full gray beard, leather jacket and jeans. He resembled a biker Bill Murray.

When the two were first paired together it was questionable whether it would work out, being that they were so different. Jeremiah was more quiet and by-the-book. Jonah was a prankster and off the cuff. The truth was, they complemented each other. Jeremiah kept Jonah grounded when need be, and Jonah kept things interesting and amusing. He hadn't kept only Jeremiah in stitches, but whole office. That's right: Angels had a sense of humor, too.

One of Jonah's pet peeves was conceit. One time a beautiful woman was on a date in a fancy restaurant on Mt. Washington. She wore a form fitting red dress and high heels. She put her nose up to everyone in the establishment, from the waiter to her gentleman companion. She wanted everyone to notice her. Just for kicks, Jonah gave the lady gas pains so bad that she couldn't hold them in. She had a look of horror on her face as she stood up from the table and began tooting loudly from behind, as she scurried bowlegged the whole way to the ladies room. Her date sat wide mouthed at a loss for words. Jeremiah and Jonah were sitting at a table nearby. You could've heard a pin drop until Jonah exclaimed, "Not so high and mighty now, is she?" All of the patrons started giggling including Jonah and Jeremiah. It may not have been the kind of recognition she was looking for, but people did take notice for sure.

Jeremiah regained his composure, and then said, "I thought we were here to head off a choking incident?"

"Yes, we are, but why not kill two birds with one stone, so to speak? A little humility has never hurt anyone," Jonah replied.

"Agreed," said Jeremiah.

Back in the present day, Jeremiah and Jonah were standing on the corner of Grant and Sixth Streets. They had an assignment coming up in ten minutes at the intersection. Jonah had a little time to kill before their task. Two men were talking to each other on the sidewalk, next to the angel partners. Both men were wearing bad toupees. Jonah decided to have a little fun. As one man talked, a slight breeze blew the other man's toupee in unison to his words. As his friend replied, the other's hair would in turn reciprocate. It was like their hair was having a conversation with each other. Jeremiah busted out laughing, while Jonah stood straight-faced. Neither of the walking souls noticed the other's talking toupee.

Jeremiah regained his composure, "Okay, come on now. It's almost time."

A young man was walking down Sixth Street toward the intersection. He was wearing ear buds and his MP3 player was too loud for him to hear anything other than his music. He was daydreaming when he approached the intersection and the *Do Not Walk* sign started flashing. A car was already accelerating through the intersection and the young man was about to step into its path. Jeremiah reached out, grabbed his arm and pulled him back onto the sidewalk. It startled the kid. He pulled his arm from Jeremiah's grasp, yanked his ear buds out, seemingly irritated, and said, "Whoa, what the hell are you doing, Mister?" Jeremiah and Jonah smiled at the kid, then walked away without a word. As the young man realized what had happened, and how the mystery man had just saved his life, he turned to apologize and thank Jeremiah, but Jeremiah was gone. He turned the volume down on his MP3 player and promised himself to pay more attention to the lights.

The partners were walking back to the office when Jeremiah grinned at Jonah and said, "One of these days you're going to get us sent to Angel Resources." He was reflecting on the talking hairpieces.

"It's all in good fun. Besides, who else keeps you entertained like me?" Jonah replied.

Jeremiah patted Jonah on the shoulder, nodded and smiled as the two walked through town.

Jonah had been sent to Angel Resources once before, back in December of 1972. Even when he was at the west coast office, Jonah had always been a Pittsburgh Steelers fan. Pittsburgh and Oakland were in a division playoff game that year. The Raiders led the Steelers 7-6 with twenty-two seconds left in the game. Terry Bradshaw threw the ball to "Frenchy" Fuqua, but when Raiders safety Jack Tatum and Fuqua collided, the ball flew back into the air. Franco Harris snatched up the ball before it hit the ground, maneuvered through Oakland's defense and ran for a touchdown to win the game. The play was branded the Immaculate Reception. Franco would be remembered for the historic play. Although Franco didn't know it, he'd had a little help from Jonah. Angel Resources were not amused with Jonah's involvement in the football game. It was made clear to Jonah that he was not to get involved in sporting outcomes again. Jonah humbly agreed without hesitation.

The Angel Resources office was located on the ninety-ninth floor of the building. It took up a small portion of the floor outside the auditorium. There were only a few employees working in the office. There was an A.R. Director, Assistant Director, and a receptionist. Most times they were able to resolve any problems without getting the C.E.O. involved. The angels were more than happy to oblige that scenario as well.

The auditorium was set up like the inside of a spectacular church, with enough pews to seat all of the employees working at C.O.A. There was a loft with a magnificent mahogany pipe organ and seating for a choir of angels. The ceiling was stunningly painted with images from the Bible. A huge diamond chandelier hung from the center of the room which reflected numerous shades of light on the auditorium. All of the wooden pews and the columns were hand carved pieces of art. There was a brilliant altar at the head of the auditorium, complete with statues, candles, and decorations. The auditorium was used for holding church services as well as C.O.A. employee meetings. All of the angels enjoyed getting together in the auditorium. It was their favorite time together.

***

Gabriel and Sarah had made progress with their situation regarding Project Lost Faith. The walking souls that they were working on had befriended the couple. Gabriel had helped the men with minor repairs around their houses. It was always good to know someone handy when you owned a home. While helping them with the repairs, Gabriel would bring up subtle moral and religious views. He did it in a way as not to seem pushy. Gabriel mainly explained how he lived his life in hopes that it would make the men want to be better people. Sarah used the same approach with the wives and girlfriends of the men. They worked well together. They did not judge people. That was not their job. They would merely offer suggestions to the walking souls. In the end, it was their decision how they wished to live their lives. The team's position was to mentor, and if possible, make them want to improve their way of living. It was better for the people and their community. The two angels had invited three couples for a small dinner party the following evening and all had accepted. They would have to prepare a game plan for the evening.

The four teams of angels that were assigned to the convention center had finished their work on the building and returned to the office. They had timed it so that no one knew they had been working in the basement. Security guards had watched them as they came in and left, but never gave it a second thought. They were used to seeing maintenance workers roaming the building. One brief glance and the guards were back to their crossword puzzles. The four teams were discussing the foundation repairs and eagerly awaiting another assignment.

After a short lull in afternoon action, the evening rush hour was approaching. There would be no shortage of work for the angels as people with short tempers and lack of patience made their way home from a hard day's labor.

CHAPTER 3

C.O.A. had two corporate offices in the U.S. The east coast office was located in Pittsburgh, as you already know. The west coast office was located in San Francisco, and overlooked the Golden Gate Bridge. Both buildings were an exact replica of each other. There were smaller satellite offices spread throughout the country. Although the satellite offices were smaller, they were no less important. Many times, angels from the corporate offices supplied help to the smaller offices as needed. Angels could also be transferred within offices depending on the necessity, as was the case when Jonah was reassigned. More often than not, there was no advance notice. Jonah was advised of his departure fifteen minutes in advance. Luckily, angels had no baggage to worry about, and there was no need for goodbyes. They knew they would all see each other again.

All walking souls had a guardian angel assigned to them. Although those angels were part of the big picture, they were always with their unique walking soul in the field. They checked in from time to time, or one of the angels would check in on them. Nonetheless, they were in constant contact with the overall operation. The corporate and satellite offices were used for the big picture, such as project deployment.

The night before had been busy on both coasts as usual. It was a new day and in Pittsburgh, new project leaders were busy handing out assignments. The previous day's project leaders were working in the field. Michael and Mary had been dispatched to the parkway east, where a walking soul was too busy reading a text to pay attention to the road. The team drained the young man's cell battery in time for him to see the stopped traffic up ahead.

Jonah and Jeremiah were on pedestrian duty again. An elderly woman who desperately needed cataract surgery was having trouble with the glare from the sun. She could only see shadows, and the oncoming cars were hard to make out. Jonah and Jeremiah walked the woman across the intersection while they carried on a conversation. Jeremiah informed her that an eye surgeon's office was directly in front of where they stood. After a brief assurance that the surgery was nothing to worry about, the woman decided to go in and make an appointment with the doctor. As she disappeared into the building, Jonah and Jeremiah followed behind some people walking down Wood Street.

Jonah pointed to a young man walking directly in front of them. The guy had headphones on with his music blaring. He was wearing his jeans halfway off of his hips. Two gorgeous young women were heading in his direction. He smiled as he caught their eye. Just at that moment his shoelaces were magically untied. As he bent down to address the situation, his trousers slipped to his ankles, revealing colorful underwear that read, *Be My Valentine.* Humiliated now, the young man quickly retrieved his pants while he turned to look at the two girls that he had tried to impress. The girls were giggling and shaking their heads as they walked on their way. The young man sped up his pace with one hand tightly hanging onto his trousers. Jeremiah turned his attention to Jonah with a smile, waiting for a response to the latest situation.

With a somber face, Jonah looked at Jeremiah, and said, "Mom always told me, make sure you have on clean underwear, because you never know when you might be in an accident, but those boxers were just an accident waiting to happen!"

"Who has more fun than people?" Jeremiah asked.

"We do!" Jonah replied.

Gabriel and Sarah were going over the plan for their upcoming dinner engagement with the neighbors. In between talking sports and home improvements, Gabriel would sneak the importance of family values into the conversation. Sarah could entwine faith in God while discussing the latest fashions and home décor. The team already knew the favorite foods of their guests. Once they had enjoyed their preferred feast, the rest would be a cinch. The two were busy adjusting furniture and knick-knacks to ensure that the guests would feel comfortable and at home when they arrived. After dinner, Gabriel would gather the men in the game room, which was full of Pirate, Steeler, and Penguin memorabilia. Sarah and her visitors would adjourn to the family room to chat.

Jeremiah and Jonah returned to the office at C.O.A. They walked into the conference room and before they could take a seat, Joseph called out to them. Joseph was the project leader of the day along with his partner Magdalene. Joseph told the team that he had an assignment for the two at a nursing home on the South Side. Jeremiah nodded, took a slip of paper from Joseph and the partners left the office once again.

The Sunny Day Nursing Home was located on a side street adjacent to Carson Street. Jeremiah and Jonah signed in with the receptionist.

"We're here to visit Rose Light," Jeremiah announced.

"Yes Sir, I'll take you to her," the receptionist replied. "She is in the activities room. I think she will be happy to have visitors." She smiled as she motioned toward Mrs. Light. Jeremiah thanked the receptionist as she returned to her duties. The team looked around the room to see most of the people enjoying an array of activities. Some were playing bingo, others sang along with a volunteer pianist, and some were just talking in small groups. Rose Light was sitting by herself in a corner. She was missing her husband, who had passed away less than six months earlier. She was a quiet woman and hadn't made a lot of friends at the facility. Rose was eighty-two and had been married to her husband, Earl, for sixty years. Her two children visited as much as they could, but both worked and had busy lives of their own. Rose was lonesome. Jeremiah and Jonah were there when Earl Light passed, and helped him with the transition. That was one of the reasons that the team had been picked for this assignment. He was a good husband and father who believed in God and loved his family. It was just his time to leave. Angels never questioned such things. Everyone had a time and a place that they left their earthly body, and that was Earl's time. Rose was not afraid of death. Her problem was that she had been with Earl for so long in life that she didn't know how to live her life without him.

Jonah strolled toward Rose with Jeremiah trailing. Jonah gestured to the chairs on both sides of Rose and asked, "Do you mind if we join you?"

Rose was startled because she had been daydreaming when the two approached her.

"I'm sorry. Please do." She held her hand toward one of the chairs.

"I am Jonah and this is my friend Jeremiah," Jonah said.

"Hello. My name is Rose. Rose Light."

"Well what a beautiful name for an attractive young woman like yourself," Jonah replied and Rose blushed with that remark.

"It is nice to meet you Rose," Jeremiah added.

"It is very nice to meet you both as well," Rose responded.

"So Rose, you don't look very happy, is something troubling you darling?" Jonah asked.

"I am just missing my husband, Earl," Rose said. Jeremiah handed Rose a handkerchief to wipe a tear from her eye and said, "Why don't you tell us about him?"

Jeremiah and Jonah listened attentively as Rose poured her heart out to the team. They consoled her when she needed it, but more than anything, she just needed to vent to someone. The partners reminded her that she would see Earl again, and she believed that in her heart. After she let it all out and she had a good cry, they talked about all of the good memories she had regarding Earl. She showed Jeremiah and Jonah pictures of her husband, daughters and grandchildren. She felt much better. She told the partners that the visit from two strangers was just what she needed, but they had already known. An hour had passed since the team came to visit and they knew that Rose was feeling much better. The pianist was still playing, but running out of steam and so were the residents. Jonah stood up and offered his hand to Rose as he said, "C'mon Rose, let's show these kids how to cut a rug!" She took his hand and they danced to an old Frank Sinatra tune, which got everyone else re-energized including the piano player. Even Jeremiah took a dance partner. Once everybody was worn out on the makeshift dance floor, it was time for the pair to head back to the office. All of the residents and aides thanked Jeremiah and Jonah for the exciting afternoon. Rose kissed them both on the cheek, thanked them for the visit. She put her hand on each of their shoulders and softly whispered, "The two of you have been heaven sent angels."

"Well, aren't you just the sweetest thing!" Jonah winked at Rose, then he and Jeremiah departed the Sunny Days Nursing Home.

As the two walked along, Jonah said, "I don't know if it was such a good idea to get the old folks wound up like that before dinner. Oh well, at least they should have worked up an appetite!"

Jeremiah sometimes forgot how good Jonah was at his job, in between all of the horsing around.

Back at the East End of town, the dinner party that Gabriel and Sarah hosted had gone on without a hitch. Everyone enjoyed the meal and each other's company. The walking souls had listened with open minds as the team talked about how important faith in God and family values were in their lives. Their guests saw how happy and grounded they were and it made them want that in their lives as well. The evening was a great success with the neighbors. A few more visits together with some tweaks here and there, then it would be time for the team to move into another neighborhood.

CHAPTER 4

As was previously mentioned, people died every day. It wasn't for the C.O.A. employees to decide who lived and who died. They were given assignments, which were handed down from the C.E.O. to the Project Leader, then to the workers. No matter what, they were to stick to the assignment at hand. Many times, such as in the case of Earl Light, their job had been only to help in the walking soul's transition and comfort the person during the event.

For all the good C.O.A. did, there were definite challenges. One of those challenges was the evil forces they would deal with. In addition to human wickedness, there were also non-human forces. They were sometimes called the Downtrodden. Mostly they were referred to as Broken Angels, or just the Broken. These were Lucifer's faction. The Broken could blend in with people just like the C.O.A. angels. The walking soul would see either one as a normal person. One thing that the Broken could not hide from the C.O.A. were their eyes. When one of the Broken walked among people, their eyes were revealed as blood red, only to the C.O.A. team. In contrast, the C.O.A. employee's eyes shone bright white to the Downtrodden. Like they say, the eyes are the window to the soul.

When the Broken came in contact with C.O.A., they tried to hide their eyes. One may have worn a baseball hat or hoodie over their brow. They usually had on dark glasses with their head down. They tried to avoid eye contact at all cost with C.O.A. employees. They tried to stay hidden at all times to the opposition. C.O.A. employees were trained to watch for the Downtrodden at all times and they knew most of their tell signs. Normally the C.O.A. did not hide their eyes from the Broken. They had nothing to conceal. The Broken on the other hand didn't want to give away any trade secrets. They tried to avoid publicizing their whereabouts to the angels. During special circumstances that called for concealment, the C.O.A. were able to turn off their glowing eyes.

Like C.O.A., Lucifer and his cohorts had corporate offices as well. H.T. Enterprises was the name on his building, which stood for Hostile Takeover. The west coast office was located in the heart of Hollywood, on Sunset Blvd. One reason Lucifer preferred the location was because most people came there to find fortune and fame. Many of those same people were susceptible to temptation and greed. The east coast office was located in lower Manhattan at Exchange Place. Lucifer was fond of the name. Just like the west coast location, it was polluted with greed and power hungry corporations. In either atmosphere, it wasn't hard to find people willing to do whatever it took to get what they wanted, and the Broken were eager to oblige them.

In their true form, the Broken had two sets of wings, but the wings were blood red in unison with their eyes. They had a sinister aura about them that was similar to a murky cloud. They had thick bushy eyebrows with cold threatening facial expressions and gray skin, as if all the blood ran directly to their eyes and wings. If walking souls could have seen them, it would frighten them beyond repair. Lucifer was similar in demeanor, but with bright red skin. He spewed steam from his ears and nose that would put you in mind of a bull snorting on a cold day. He also breathed out flames when he spoke, which made him even more intimidating. Even his followers avoided eye contact with him when possible.

The good and evil had met up with each other many times at crime scenes. Beyond the police tape, C.O.A. employees could spot the beady red eyes of the Downtrodden throughout the crowd of onlookers. Most often, they were merely gloating or looking for new recruits. It was an eerie sight, especially at night, but that was when they liked to operate. They did their best work in the dark of the night.

Even the office buildings at Hostile Takeover Enterprises were dark and dreary. They were made of cold black steel and had no windows on the outside walls. There were menacing figurines that resembled dragons, snakes and reptiles with wings, atop the seventy-five story buildings that seemed to be guarding the structures. The buildings were surrounded by a nasty green bubbling liquid that could only be imagined coming from a horrible nuclear accident. The liquid was filled with four-eyed monsters that were used as a deterrent for inquisitive C.O.A. employees. The only ways in or out were a thick metal door at the front of the building that lowered over the moat, and a smaller door on the roof of the building.

Inside the structure, Lucifer's cronies had no cubicles or privacy. Their small desks were crowded together in the center of each office floor. As you could imagine, there was not much trust in the offices and Lucifer kept his eyes on all of his employees. With no windows in the building, it was always hot and stuffy. The only light within the building came from dim florescent fixtures in the ceiling, which caused a constant ominous humming sound that resonated throughout the building, due to the ballasts in the lights. The fluorescent lighting seemed to accentuate the gray complexion of the workers inside, like death warmed over. Overall, the offices resembled the worst sweatshop imaginable in some third world country, and backstabbing was a prerequisite.

Unlike the corporate structure at C.O.A., H.T. Enterprises had a management flowchart. Only the most ruthless of employees were able to climb the corporate ladder. Lucifer's right hand thug was Covah, and he was as terrifying as Satan himself. He oversaw both the east and west coast offices and Lucifer trusted him more than any of his other employees. There were no partners at Hostile Takeover, which was also in contrast to C.O.A. All of the Broken worked alone, or in packs when necessary. There were no project leaders, but there were foremen, supervisors, directors, and board members. Everyone had a boss; there were no equals at H.T. Enterprises. Soahc was the dictator of the east coast office and Mehyam was in charge of the west coast office. Both of these tyrants were handpicked by Lucifer and they ruled with iron fists.

New covert commands were passed down from Lucifer and were hand delivered to each corporate office by Covah in the afternoon. Each executive was to put them into motion without delay. Both anxiously agreed, then ordered a board meeting to convene within the hour. Activity started thriving throughout each of the buildings.

On the east end of Pittsburgh, Gabriel had tried to call one of his former clients, Tim Rice, but Tim hadn't returned any of his calls in the past week or so. Both Gabriel and Sarah believed that Tim would be the perfect candidate to help the team out on the new project. Tim was friendly, energetic and outgoing. He also seemed to have responded favorably to the team's ideas and values. However, the team hadn't heard from Tim in a while, which seemed out of character for him. On that day, Gabriel and Sarah decided to go by Tim's house to make sure that everything was alright.

Tim's apartment was located in a lower income neighborhood in East Pittsburgh. Most of the residents that lived in the community were hard working people who took pride in their homes. The yards and the houses, although older, seemed to be well maintained.

When Gabriel and Sarah had come within one-hundred yards of Tim's apartment, they noticed someone exiting Tim's place. Gabriel recognized the man right away, and he groaned loud enough for Sarah to notice. When she realized who it was, she grimaced, which followed suit with Gabriel's displeasure.

The one who had been responsible for the team's sudden frustration was Seil, a recruiter for the Broken. Amongst walking souls, Seil appeared as a good looking and confident individual. He donned a million dollar smile and silver tongue. He was always dressed impeccably in an expensive suit, shoes and a well-groomed haircut. It was all part of his act to exude success. He had continually sniffed around Gabriel and Sarah's business. Seil had been an annoyance to the team longer than they cared to admit.

Without a word to Sarah, Gabriel crossed the street and made a beeline for the recruiter. Sarah quickly followed behind. Seil had noticed Gabriel before the two met on the corner. Seil remained cool as could be, but noticed Gabriel's troubled demeanor.

"Well, if it isn't my old chum Gabriel and his sidekick," Seil grinned. "You're looking a little tired there buddy. They say eight hours is good for that."

"You're looking good Seil. You remind me of an ice cold glass of milk on a warm day, until you take a big gulp, only to find out that it was spoiled."

Seil extended his arms out and said, "Now that hurts Gabe, after all we've been through."

"Okay boys, play nice," Sarah added. "Why are you here, Seil?"

"Just visiting a friend," Seil continued, as he lit a cigarette. "He's been down on his luck and needed a job. I was just being neighborly, Girl Wonder."

"You need to stay away from Tim," Gabriel retorted.

18

"God gave free will, Gabe. Tim is a big boy. He knows what he needs. Besides, just because you guys have to play by the rules, doesn't mean I have to."

Seil saw that Gabriel's face had turned flush, so he added insult to misery, "Careful there Gabe, your coloring is starting to resemble our side!"

"Let's go Gabriel," Sarah tugged on his sleeve, "it's not worth it."

"This isn't over Seil," Gabriel spouted as he turned to leave.

"You know where to find me, Gabe," Seil responded as he stamped out his cigarette on the ground, then walked away.

Sarah recommended to Gabriel that it would be better to postpone their visit with Tim. They could return later, after a cool down period. Gabriel agreed that would be best. Seil beeped the horn and waved to the team as he drove by in a brand new Lincoln MKZ.

CHAPTER 5

Back at C.O.A., things were moving along as usual. Employees were exiting and returning from assigned tasks. The afternoon seemed no different than any normal workday, except for the presence of a few military workers. Their presence was not usually seen at the corporate office unless a threat of some kind had been detected. With only a few of the armed forces in attendance, it could just be a precaution. To the workers, it seemed odd to see any military presence, given the lack of sightings of the opposition within the last week or so.

It was hard not to notice one of God's Army occupying the building. Only the fiercest warriors were handpicked by God to serve. Those fighting machines had at least one foot more height than all other angels, and had no body fat. They were pure muscle, with an extra set of wings extending from each calf. All three sets of wings were used as a shield which protected them from head to toe. Each one carried a staff at all times and it was the only weapon they needed. The very sight of one of these combatants was intimidating.

Normally, the army personnel were out in various satellite offices all over the country. When the need arose for a strong military presence, the army would take over the command center in one or both corporate offices. The head of the west coast army was General Luke. General James was in charge of the east coast. Both leaders had been in their appointed positions for as long as any C.O.A. employees could remember.

Jonah and Jeremiah had returned to C.O.A. from their visit with Rose at the nursing home. The first thing they noticed was Sergeants Mathew and

Peter, who stood at attention as they entered the lobby of the office. Jonah stopped briefly between the massive guards, glanced at each of them and remarked in an authoritative voice, "As you were, gentlemen."

Neither of the servicemen acknowledged Jonah, they kept their eyes straight forward, so he shrugged his shoulders and moved on. Jeremiah kept his gaze to the floor and followed behind Jonah through the lobby. The team entered their second floor office and before they had caught their breath, Joseph handed the team a new assignment. When they left the premises Jonah saluted the two-man unit, then watched briefly for a hint of a smile, not that he had expected one. After being thwarted twice, the partners were on their way to Mt. Washington.

At least twice a year, some daring adventurer decided that he could climb Mount Washington. They were usually teenagers with more brawn than brains. Although a few had successfully made the trek, most needed to be rescued. The hillside was very steep and slippery. An incline traversed the eighty degree slope, and that was the only thing that should. More often than not, the kids were barely able to continue the climb past halfway. On that particular day, two friends had made it to sixty-five percent of the grade and were barely hanging on. The incline operators usually informed the police and fire department, but the two daring individuals were not in the operators' view between the overgrown shrubs.

The boys didn't notice the team until they were almost on top of them. Both kids were startled by their presence.

"Whoa, where did you guys come from?" one of the boys jerked as he hollered out.

"Take it easy, we're here to help you down," Jeremiah answered, holding his palms up.

"No way. We can make it," the other boy disputed, not quite believing his own words.

"Look at your arms shaking," Jonah replied. "You won't make it to Grandview Avenue my friend. You will be lucky to climb ten more yards before rolling down and landing like road kill on Carson Street."

After briefly glancing down the hill and having considered Jonah's scenario, both boys agreed to accept help from the team. Jeremiah tied a rope to a beam from the track of the incline and tossed the slack below them. Both boys were trembling from fatigue. Jonah and Jeremiah steadied each boy in front of them as they slowly descended the slope. When they reached the road below, both boys laid back onto the ground. They were completely exhausted and closed their eyes for a moment. When they opened their eyes, the team had disappeared.

"Where did they go?" one boy asked the other nervously.

"I have no idea!" the other friend replied, as he scanned the area. "Let's just get out of here."

"You don't have to tell me twice," his friend agreed, then the two began strolling back down Carson Street.

From their seats on the Duquesne Incline, Jonah and Jeremiah watched the two boys march down the street. The partners decided to take in the scenic view of the city since they were already there. "That will give them something to talk about for a while, huh?" Jeremiah said.

"Do you think they are wondering how we showed up there, or where we disappeared to?" Jonah asked.

"Both," Jeremiah replied, "but I have a feeling they will keep it to themselves!" The team laughed as the incline gradually made its way up the mountain.

After a brief meeting with their project leaders, Gabriel and Sarah agreed that their time spent in the East End was coming to a close. The team was happy, for the most part, with the results and had made great progress with the neighbors. Movers from the warehouse in the Strip District would be sent to pick up their furniture and take it to another home in the North Hills where the team would start over with new clients. The partners would explain to their East End friends that Gabriel was being transferred up north. They would exchange phone numbers so they could keep in touch with each other. The team always left a phone number for their clients and many kept in touch with them. Usually the clients would go about their lives just fine, but sometimes they needed more mentoring along the way.

Once again, Gabriel and Sarah returned to East Pittsburgh to check in with Tim Rice. When Tim answered the door, he didn't seem so enthused to see the team. Sarah had noticed stacked boxes in the living room. After some small talk, she asked, "Are you moving out, Tim?"

At first, Tim was apprehensive, then replied, "Yes, a friend of mine offered me a new position, training to be a trader for a commodities company. It is pretty good money, so I'll be moving to a nicer place in a few weeks, close to town."

Gabriel asked, "Would your friend's name be Seil?"

"Yes," Tim was surprised, "do you know him?"

"Yes, I know of him. Be careful, Tim. Seil's company has been investigated by the F.T.C. on a few occasions," Gabriel warned.

Tim quickly changed the subject, "So, what can I do for you two?"

"We haven't heard from you, so we wanted to check in." Sarah smiled.

"We thought you might be interested in leading a project that we've been working on?" Gabriel rejoined.

Tim replied sheepishly, "I don't know, Gabriel. I'm not going to have much time, with the new job and all."

"Congratulations on the job, Tim!" Sarah tried to lighten the mood, "Think about our offer, and let us know if you find some time."

Tim thanked the team for stopping, then went back to work in his apartment.

At that point, Gabriel and Sarah had their doubts regarding their plans for Tim and the project; they would revisit him at another time. The team would need to consider finding another walking soul with leadership skills.

Operation Lost Faith had been stepping up efforts, due to a stagnant atmosphere among walking souls regarding religion. The opposition had been placing a lot of negativity in the air. Recruiters like Seil sometimes made it tough for Gabriel and Sarah to keep the walking souls on the right path. Especially when they could be easily tempted. As Seil had previously mentioned, the Broken didn't have to play by the same rules as C.O.A. employees. The Broken preyed on the young people too. They would try to win them over to their end of the spectrum by any means. The Broken would spew lies about God and they took advantage of certain people's undecided views. Lately, they had tried to make it look cool not to believe. Sadly, it worked with some young people who were easily swayed, or not willing to open their hearts to His word. The Broken used many resources to help spread their message, such as bars, nightclubs and drug corners. There were atheist and agnostic groups online as well. There was nowhere the Broken wouldn't go to find new recruits, especially when people were at their most vulnerable points. As a matter of fact, that was what they were hoping for. Luckily, C.O.A. employees were willing to go the distance as well, and had been making up ground, which hadn't sat well with H.T. Enterprises.

CHAPTER 6

It was the beginning of a long night at HT Enterprises as well. During the afternoon board meeting it had been decided to assemble a few platoons from Lucifer's army at the east and west coast offices and keep them on standby. The board members would reconvene behind closed doors later in the evening, to fine tune their strategy. All workers were confined to the building until further notice. H.T. Enterprises was on lockdown. Lucifer didn't want any leaks reaching outside of their walls.

The soldiers had been held in conference rooms at both buildings awaiting further instructions. They were unsettling, massive beings. Their skin was dark, scaly and hard, which resembled a reptile. Their feet were long and wide with sharp talons similar to those of a falcon. They had two sets of red wings and carried a scepter. They were a terrifying vision indeed, and even more so in a multitude.

The conference room at H.T. Enterprises was as dreary and depressing as the rest of the building. It had cramped auditorium seating, much like that of an old movie theater. There were no windows, which kept in unison with the rest of the building's décor. There was somewhat better lighting, but most of it was directed at the stage. In the center of the stage was a throne for Lucifer. There was also a podium with a few folding chairs off to the side, which were reserved for his top leaders.

The secret board meeting had been in session for over an hour and would be wrapped up shortly. The blinds were closed with guards posted outside the entrance. The remainder of the employees were on their respective floors awaiting instruction. Some were gathering information on their computers, while others were sitting quietly at their desks. There was to be no phone communication until further notice. The workers were busy on the computers, researching locations on Google Earth that were given by the foremen.

In the H.T. conference room, some members of the platoons had a crap game going on. Others were playing cards, trying to pass the time. A few groups of soldiers were making small talk, but the majority of the units were quietly meditating. It was the quiet before the storm and each had their own way of relaxing while they waited.

When Jonah and Jeremiah had returned once again to C.O.A., they noticed more chatter than usual between the workers. The employees were talking amongst themselves about the abnormal movement of employees, as they came and went from H.T. Enterprises on both coasts. Project leaders at C.O.A. were advised to keep the employees close to home, in anticipation of the possibility of an event that required fast action. They were ordered to keep their eyes and ears open for any sign of an uprising. C.O.A. operatives had confirmed the unusual activity in the nemesis camp. It was to be a long night at C.O.A., with all hands on deck.

Meanwhile, Jeremiah had noticed General James passing through and nudged Jonah, then nodded to the General. He was on his way upstairs to a meeting. The commander was followed, not far behind, by Sergeants Mathew and Peter, along with their two platoons of soldiers. All of the soldiers stepped in perfect unison, in pairs of two behind the sergeants. Each one donned a very serious face and kept their eyes forward. They were headed to the Command Center on the ninety-eighth floor and would be briefed by General James, after a conference meeting with the C.E.O. and the west coast office.

Inside each of the meeting rooms were the respective Generals, along with three high ranking field operatives and two project leaders that had been chosen earlier that afternoon. In all, eight people on either coast were in attendance. They were communicating via satellite video. The C.E.O. was elsewhere, but on speakerphone.

"So, what do we know so far?" A loud booming voice bellowed over the speaker.

General James motioned to the principal operative to take the lead.

Mark cleared his throat, then introduced himself as the head of the Intelligence Department, which was located on floors ninety and ninety-one. "As you know, H.T. has been quiet for the last few days and they are currently on lockdown for the moment. We have been informed that a covert board meeting is taking place as we speak. Many employees have been uploading several mapped locations on Google Earth. Most of which are meant to be diversions, but the majority of concentration seems to be centralized near Frederick, Maryland on the east coast and Las Vegas on the west coast."

"Do you have an idea of their plans?" the voice boomed from the speaker again.

A west coast operative on the video screen, piped up, "We feel that they will be targeting some mode of transportation."

"How soon before we know more?" General James asked.

"We have operatives in the field at H.T. and they have guaranteed us more facts within the half-hour."

"Let the operators do their job and we will reconvene in thirty minutes. Good job everyone," the C.E.O. replied, then the phone line disconnected.

General Luke spoke up, "James, contact me if anything changes, otherwise we will see you in thirty."

"You got it Luke, talk to you shortly," General James replied, and the video feed was gone.

The eight employees emptied out of the conference rooms. General James and General Luke had gone to fill in their platoon leaders on the latest findings from the meeting, and to remind the men to be ready to be deployed, following the next meeting. When General James entered the conference room, the men had been patiently sitting quietly, but jumped to attention as he entered the room. None of them were fooling around. They were all staying focused and clearing their minds of anything else besides the upcoming mission.

General James told the soldiers that he would return shortly with orders, and then left the room. The General walked back down one floor and returned to the command center, where he waited for the others to arrive with new intelligence.

The players started trickling back into the meeting room; about five minutes shy of the half-hour time limit. Everyone took their seats and the video feed was called up. The C.E.O. was also back on the speaker phone.

"What is the conclusion, Mark?" God spoke first.

"Well, Sir, we looked for airports in the vicinity of the area where the highest activity had taken place on the queries. Although airports are not extremely far away, they are not directly near the closest points of interest for H.T. What we did find were train tracks in line of both west coast and east coast targets," Mark explained.

"There is a commuter train running from Chicago to Needles. It is called the Southwest Chief," General Luke exclaimed.

"The Capitol Limited train runs between Washington, D.C. and Pittsburgh, at about the same time," General James replied.

"Exactly," Mark chimed in, "that is what we think they are targeting. Either one or both commuter trains. We are figuring a fifty mile radius near Fredrick, Maryland in the east and Needles, California in the west."

"What time will the trains arrive in each area?" General James requested from Mark.

"The E.T.A. is eleven o'clock eastern standard time, eight pacific," Mark replied.

"That gives us about an hour," General Luke said, glancing at his watch.

A voice bellowed from the speakerphone again, "Generals, let's set out right away, notify the troops and get them in the air."

"Copy that, Sir," both commanders replied on the way out of the rooms.

Each General hurried up the steps to prepare the platoon leaders. Within five minutes the angels were on their way to the separate locations.

By ten-fifteen, the angel warriors were in place, starting in D.C. on one end, and twenty-five miles past Fredrick, working their way toward each other. Each platoon was inspecting the tracks and would meet in the middle. Lookouts were watching for the beady red eyes as they moved along. Lucifer's army would be as careful as possible not to let the C.O.A. notice their light. The platoon leaders were notified of heavy traffic leaving the H.T. headquarters and warned to watch for the combatants.

The troops on the west coast were busy conducting the same operation between Needles and Las Vegas. They, too, had been informed of movement out of H.T. in San Francisco. Both groups of the C.O.A. knew timing would be crucial. They were moving as fast as possible to head off any intrusions.

On the top of the C.O.A. buildings on both coasts was the office of the C.E.O. To look at the outside of the building, the top floor resembled a giant sphere. It was made of thick glass. No metal whatsoever. Inside the office would put you in mind of a giant snow globe, minus the snow. There was a three-hundred-sixty degree spectacular view, which was like looking through binoculars. From this office God kept an eye on His world. As far as offices go, it was very humble. There was no desk, computer or phone. The only pieces of furniture in the room were two chairs. There was one for the C.E.O. and one for a visitor. All office visits were one on one. The C.E.O. could change the view with a blink of His eye, like you would change the channel on your T.V. At that moment, He sat quietly and watched from an aerial view over Frederick, Maryland as His soldiers worked.

CHAPTER 7

Things had indeed been full of activity inside the H.T. Enterprises. Lucifer's army platoons were dispatched from the office buildings and their whereabouts were kept quiet from the majority of H.T. employees, except for the high ranking managers. Unlike C.O.A., there was not much trust within the company and confidence amongst employees was not a strong suit with H.T. When a member of the staff was picked for an assignment, they could be sure that other eyes were upon them. They were ready to snitch on co-workers without hesitation, if it helped them climb to a higher position on the company flow chart. The C.E.O. preferred this method of promotion from within. He thought it kept his employees on their toes.

H.T. soldiers had been leaving both office buildings here and there, for a few hours. They didn't want to leave at the same time, as they tried not to draw suspicion. They were unaware that C.O.A. was already hot on their trail. The soldiers were close to Gaithersburg when they saw the first sign of a red twinkle. It was just for a moment, but the lookouts had caught a glimpse. The angels had been using their staffs like spotlights. As fast as they had spotted the opposition, they disappeared. H.T. soldiers preferred to work in quiet and darkness, but it was too late. The C.O.A. knew they were close on their tails.

The Capitol Limited was crowded, almost at full capacity. The Snowbirds were on their trip back north from Florida. Snowbird was a name given to people who spent their winters in Florida and returned back north for the summer. Most of them left before the first snowfall and resurfaced in the springtime, near Easter. With the return of the snowbirds, in addition to people visiting Washington, D.C., the commuter train was chock-full of passengers. The C.O.A. military knew they had to act fast.

A few miles from the first sighting of the H.T. army, the angels found the trouble they had been anticipating. On a hard bend, a big chunk of track had been pulled apart on one side. The fifteen foot section was just large enough for the train to slide off and leave the track. As if that wasn't bad enough, there was a forty foot drop-off on that bend. H.T. had finished their damage seconds before the angels arrived. When they took off, they didn't realize that C.O.A. troops had pushed them directly into the path of the second C.O.A. platoon. Ten angels had started working on repairs to the damaged track, while the remaining twenty continued to pursue the H.T. army. Like kicking a rabbit out of the brush toward the other hunters, the army unrelentingly guided their prey.

Now that the C.O.A. soldiers had the H.T. troops in view, they began singing battle hymns and praises as loud as they could. The boisterous mantras scared the H.T. army as much as the sight of the soldiers. Remember, Lucifer's army liked to work in silence. There was no hiding their eyes now. It had started to look like a red laser show in the sky. The C.O.A. soldiers were gaining ground on the H.T. forces. The Broken flew as fast as they could to get away from the situation. In the distance they could see a white glow. That was when they realized they were being led directly into the path of the second platoon of C.O.A. military. At that point they knew there would be a confrontation between the two armies.

On the train, most of the passengers were fading in and out of sleep. The steady rhythm of the steel wheels clicking on the rails could be a soothing sound. There were fifteen passenger cars, which held approximately forty walking souls per car, in addition to the engine and caboose. The train was roughly twelve miles from the damaged track and cruising at fifty miles per hour. The conductor had no idea what danger he was headed for.

Moments after the H.T. army had seen the second platoon of C.O.A. soldiers, the first blow was initiated. The lead angel rained down short bursts of lightning on the H.T. front line. As the fire bolt singed one of the Broken on their back, the smell of burnt flesh was in the air. Just as the train had passed under the battleground, the soldier that had taken a hit to his back fell to the ground beside the eastbound train. The armies clashed like thunder into one another. One of the walking souls on-board the locomotive had asked the conductor if he heard thunder, but he shook his head, no. The person was sickly and as previously mentioned, only very sick walking souls were able to see or hear angels. None of the other passengers heard any commotion at all.

All the while, the C.O.A. soldiers chanted and sang as they attempted to dismantle the H.T. military. The angels had all three sets of their wings wrapped around them like armor. The fire that came from the H.T. scepters was not enough to penetrate the angel's wings. It looked like a war zone as the platoons pelted lightning bolts onto the Broken. They also used the staff to block and strike down the H.T. opposition as if the weapon were a baseball bat. At least ten H.T. soldiers were lying on the ground. The remainder of the two platoons had scattered in different directions. With the H.T. soldiers now on the run, the C.O.A. units hurried back to the damaged track to assess the situation. They knew the fleeing H.T. soldiers would circle back to retrieve their wounded and return to their headquarters. There were no C.O.A. casualties.

On their return to the scene of the crime, the platoon that had chased the Broken came upon the angels that had been trying to fix the busted track. The Capitol Limited was closing in fast and the track had been destroyed beyond repair. As the locomotive rapidly closed in on the maintenance team, a new plan was put into action. The staffs of the angels would be used as a makeshift rail for the train. There was no alternative at that point. The ten employees that had been on site the whole time were lined up side by side along the track. The armed forces lay on the ground and held their staffs out and adjoined each of them from the beginning to the end of broken rail. They braced themselves as the train approached their location. The remaining soldiers were split up on either side of the train, in case they needed to guide it onto the safe rails as it went along. With all their might, the angels kept the cars as steady as they could, while they rolled over the missing rails. All fifteen passenger cars as well as the engine and caboose made it safely past the sabotaged vicinity with only one passenger aboard who realized anything out of the ordinary had happened. That passenger thought he had noticed shadows in the dark, but blamed it on exhaustion. He decided to close his eyes and get some rest.

Now that the catastrophe had been diverted near Gaithersburg, the platoons were headed back to C.O.A. headquarters. The railroad company had already been informed by an anonymous caller regarding the damaged track. Railroad employees were headed to the site, and other trains were being temporarily deflected away from the route. Now all C.O.A. attention would be switched to the west coast.

General Luke was in constant contact with his military. The two platoons had gone over the entire track from Needles to Las Vegas. They had found no problems with it whatsoever. Once they were satisfied, they turned their attention to the Southwest Chief itself. The soldiers flew in unison toward the locomotive which was now twenty miles outside of Needles. C.O.A. didn't think the H.T. evildoers would use the same modus operandi as was attempted with the east coast train. As the C.O.A. army had the train in sight, it became clear that H.T. were indeed present. The Broken had engulfed the engine car like a pack of coyotes. Some were trying to loosen bolts on the engine. Others tried to dismantle the leading vehicle in any way possible. Luckily, they were in the beginning stages of anarchy. Again the C.O.A. started chanting loudly with trumpets blaring. They succeeded in startling the H.T. warriors.

As in the eastern battle, the angels rained down lightning flashes on the H.T. militia. Others were spewing red hot metal balls that looked like oversized pumpkin balls. It was an even greater light show in the sky than the east coast battle. The angels ducked most of the retaliation that the Broken had thrown at the C.O.A. There was one soldier who had been nicked in the neck with flying shrapnel, but he was hanging in there. H.T. casualties were worse than the east coast skirmish. There were twenty five H.T. soldiers out of commission. The C.O.A. maintenance crew were able to inspect the engine and after a few minor repairs, the engine had been returned to good as new. Both missions had been a success for C.O.A. Their teamwork had proven to be a valuable asset for the corporation on that day. On the other hand, heads would roll at H.T. headquarters.

Against Sarah's urging to leave it alone for a while, Gabriel wanted to revisit Tim Rice. When Tim saw that it was Gabriel again, he wasn't happy to see him.

"Hi Tim," Sarah smiled.

"Sarah, Gabriel," Tim replied, halfheartedly, "what are you doing here again?"

Gabriel spoke up, "We were wondering, have you given any more thought to working with us?"

"Look, Gabriel, I tried to be nice. I don't want to work on your project. I don't want you coming around anymore. I don't want to see you! Is that clear enough for you? Now get the hell out of here. I have work to do!" Tim slammed the door, as Gabriel stood dumfounded. Sarah had been afraid that would happen. Her partner took everything to heart. She put her arm around Gabriel and they left without a word.

Around the corner, out of sight, Seil leaned against a wall and quietly blew smoke rings from his cigarette. He had heard the whole conversation. Truth be told, Seil was jealous of Gabriel. He saw the respect that Gabriel's coworkers had always shown him. Seil was barely acknowledged by his colleagues, and had never received approval for a job well done. There was nothing he enjoyed more than watching Gabriel's anguish when he had lost a walking soul.

CHAPTER 8

Another debriefing meeting was in progress at C.O.A. headquarters. All of the same employees were in attendance as the last meeting. Again the C.E.O. was on speaker phone and there was a video feed between the east and west coast.

"What did we learn from these two conflicts with the H.T. army?" the C.E.O. asked, once everyone was in place.

General James spoke up first, "We need to be faster with intelligence for sure. We were almost too late on the east coast." He was trying not to point fingers, but stated the obvious. "I agree," General Luke added.

"We will be more attentive going forward and will add additional employees in our department," Mark said, admitting some responsibility.

"We will do the same out here," the west coast operative replied.

"Let's learn from our mistakes. Nothing is to be taken for granted where the Broken are concerned, although I commend each and every one of you for heading off this disastrous situation." They thanked the C.E.O. for acknowledging their hard work. All personnel filed out of the meeting room and returned to their posts.

H.T. headquarters was having a totally different type of meeting. The injured employees, already aching from their recent wounds, were being beaten for losing the scuffle with C.O.A. In fact the entire platoons were being whipped, which added to their misery. They knew some of the soldiers would be sent to solitary confinement, in addition to the two beatings that they had received already. Solitary confinement for this type of punishment could be as long as five years in a dungeon without any contact whatsoever.

With as much backstabbing that went on throughout the company, you would have thought it might be a blessing. The truth was, even contact with a scoundrel was better than not talking to anyone, especially during a five year stretch. More than likely, many of the wounded soldiers would be punished in this fashion. Others that were deemed as cowards, who ran from the C.O.A. army, would also join them in their sentence. It depended on a decision made by Lucifer himself, and at the moment he was on the warpath.

With H.T. Enterprises, it wasn't about how many walking souls were killed. It was about installing fear in the minds of the walking souls. If one, or both, of these attacks had been accomplished as they were meant to be, it would have caused turmoil among the people. The first thing out of their mouths would be talk of terrorists. It would have pitted people against each other. They would have been looking over their shoulder constantly, just as was the case during 9/11. Lucifer thrived on that type of fear. People questioned God. Why didn't he prevent such a horrific accident? It was just the edge that H.T. needed to try and sway people over to the dark side. Nothing helped the H.T. cause more than doubt, fear and uncertainty. With Project Lost Faith having worked in favor of the C.O.A., Lucifer thought that it was the perfect time to win over more prospects as his followers. Given his defeat on that day, he would need to come back with an even more despicable plan. In the meantime, a slip of paper was handed to Soahc with a list of unlucky names to be placed in solitary confinement. Soahc informed the east and west coast leaders of the unfortunate soldiers that were to be incarcerated. They would meet later to discuss new recruits to replace the doomed soldiers.

For the time being, the military presence had been released back to their assigned offices and the Generals left C.O.A. as well, but were ordered to be on standby in case of another uprising. Everything was back to normal for the moment, with the exception of additional personnel being assigned to the operative teams on both coasts, and additional agents being assigned outside both office locations of the H.T. buildings, to keep an eye on the traffic in and out of their headquarters. C.O.A. computer activity had been ramped up as well, so that no slack was given to chatter among H.T. employees, no matter how mundane it appeared.

Gabriel and Sarah were closing up loose ends on the East End and were busy contacting their assigned walking souls one last time, before being moved to their new location. The movers would be at the house the next day to pack up and lug their furniture to the new house. You are probably wondering why they didn't just magically send everything to the new house like Samantha on Bewitched, but it needed to appear as normal as possible to walking souls in the area. The movers would come with a C.O.A. moving truck, complete with laborers in uniform. Everyone has known one or two neighbors that have kept an eye on all comings and goings that happen in their neighborhood. Any movement on the street, no matter how small would catch the attention of those people. If the home was just emptied without any movement in or out of the house it would look suspicious. Every precaution was taken to prevent unwanted questioning.

Gabriel couldn't get Tim Rice out of his mind. The team went to see their supervisor, Benjamin, for advice. The manager had decided to tell Gabriel a story.

"A cubic zirconia is a beautiful stone, it shines up nice and looks pretty. It can even fool some people into thinking that it is a diamond, right?"

Gabriel was confused. "What does that story have to do with anything?"

"Give me a minute," the supervisor continued. "A diamond, on the other hand, can withstand very high temperatures. It is a beautiful, resilient stone and way more valuable than a cubic zirconia. Wouldn't you agree?"

"Yes, but what is the point?" Gabriel asked.

"Okay, don't worry so much about finding a walking soul with charisma, or charm. It isn't a popularity contest. What is the name of the project?" The supervisor asked.

Gabriel responded, "Project Lost Faith."

"What is the main word?" The supervisor waited.

"Faith," Gabriel responded.

"Exactly. Find someone with strong convictions. Someone who is resilient and can take the heat. The rest will fall into place."

Sarah could see that Benjamin had made Gabriel feel somewhat better. Maybe now they could move forward and find the best walking soul for the job.

There were still assignments being handed down throughout the night, but movement had slowed immensely compared to the excitement earlier in the evening. Many of the employees had been sent out to prevent robberies. Most robberies occurred late in the evening when fewer people were on the streets. The thieves had a better chance of disappearing into the night after knocking over a convenience store and there was usually less chance of being identified by witnesses. The situations that the teams worried about most were scared, trigger happy fools that had a higher chance of shooting someone. Thieves that were high, or trying to get high were the most dangerous, because they would do what they had to do to feed their habit. Many people that were just down on their luck didn't want to hurt anyone; they were just trying to steal a few bucks to get by.

Jeremiah and Jonah had been sent to the Sunoco gas station on Forbes Avenue. A crack addict was looking for money to get a fix and he was in a bad way. The clerk of the store was a twenty-year-old girl. She was working her way through the University of Pittsburgh. She liked working nights because she could study while it was slow and there were no customers in the store. She had her head buried in a textbook, so she didn't notice when the angels entered the store, just seconds before the burglar walked in with a gun. Jeremiah and Jonah were pretending to look for snacks in the rear of the building. The intruder pulled his gun and nervously shouted at the shocked clerk. She was so scared that she didn't move or make a sound. As the robber screamed at her to fill the paper bag with cash, she became more unresponsive. She was frozen with fear, which only made the gunman more anxious. He was so engrossed with the clerk that he had no clue the team was behind him. Jeremiah rolled a can of soda across the floor toward the door. As the would be robber turned his attention and the gun toward the can, Jonah pulled a broomstick from behind his back—one that he had taken from the back room of the store. He swung the broomstick around and caught the man behind the knees and flipped him into the air like a rag doll. He landed backwards on the floor, banging his head on the can of soda which knocked him out.

"Call 911," Jonah hollered to the young clerk, "tell them to come and arrest this guy while we tie him up."

Finally, the clerk regained her composure and nervously dialed for the police.

"Thank you so much," she said, as she covered the phone, still shaking. "I don't know what would have happened if you two weren't here."

"No problem," Jeremiah replied. "We were in the neighborhood at the right time, that's all."

The team left the establishment before the police arrived, with the man unconscious and hogtied.

"That guy will have more than one headache when he wakes up in jail," Jonah said.

"Yes, but at least he will only be put away for attempted robbery and not murder," Jeremiah replied. "He may still have time to turn his life around while he's incarcerated."

With the way the clerk had shut down during the robbery, it would only have ended badly for both of the walking souls if the partners hadn't been there.

"What? No witty banter this time Jonah? You must be slipping," Jeremiah teased Jonah as the two exited the gas station.

Jonah piped up, "The only thing I can say is that I hope that child isn't majoring in Oral Communication. Could you see if she was a lawyer? That would be the shortest trial in history!"

CHAPTER 9

As was promised by Mark, C.O.A. was in the midst of strengthening the field operations. He was back in the conference room where the last meeting had occurred. At the time, he was with three employees that had been chosen to enhance the department. Most angels at C.O.A. worked in teams of two, but in some cases three seemed to click with each other. Such was the case with these associates. Their names were Sephora, Serafina, and Michaela. Between the three of them, they showed strength, intelligence and compassion. Sephora and Serafina were both African American women in their mid-fifties. Michaela was a little Italian woman in her late forties. The group had shown their expertise in fulfilling tough assignments many times over. Mark explained to the employees that they would be spending a lot of time in New York near H.T. headquarters.

Sephora was the level-headed one of the group. She had a talent for dealing with people. Her smile and warm demeanor would usually put most people at ease. Sephora had a slender build and appeared harmless, but don't let that fool you. She could scrap with the best. She was best at keeping her two teammates grounded. Serafina was the tough, strong, straightforward one. She was larger and more muscular than her two co-workers and was a loyal, no nonsense employee who always had your back. Michaela was a sarcastic, pain in the ass fireball, but had a good heart. She was the shortest and loudest, but more importantly, the most compassionate of the three. Although Michaela was extremely caring, she had no tolerance for ignorance or callous people. Just like her cohorts, she could be counted on in a crunch. Serafina and Michaela both had been known to be impatient with people at times. Serafina had a low tolerance for ignorance and Michaela could have a sassy attitude with people in general, until they got to know her. Together, these three allies formed a dynamic relationship that worked well in harmony.

Mark went on to make it clear to the trio how important their mission was to C.O.A. They would have to keep a low profile in New York City. Keeping their identity secret from the H.T. employees was vital to the mission. They needed to uncover strategies of the Broken and report back to C.O.A. with information, no matter how mundane it seemed to be. With their objectives fully understood, the group emerged from the conference room and immediately vacated the building. Their road trip was underway.

Jeremiah and Jonah were given an assignment in Wheeling, West Virginia. Jonah was happy to get out of the city for a while. The two had filled out their requisitions for transportation and had the supply group sign off. On the way through the Strip District, Jonah stopped to take a peek through the window of Primanti Brothers. Primanti's was a favored restaurant in the area among walking souls. The atmosphere of the restaurant had always intrigued Jonah. Although angels didn't need to eat to survive, they did consume food while on an assignment that required them to fit in with the walking souls.

Jonah loved to watch the cooks at Primanti's, as they piled cole slaw, french fries and tomato on top of the meat of your choice and freshly made bread. Cheese steak seemed to be the most popular sandwich. The place was always packed as the cooks hollered out, "Who ordered the cheese steak?" Someone along the back wall would raise their hand and the cook would throw a perfect spiral with the wrapped sandwich to the customer. The whole thing just tickled Jonah as he watched in awe like a small child at a circus.

Once Jeremiah was able to drag Jonah away from the storefront, the team made their way to the warehouse in the Strip, where they would pick up a few bikes. It was a nice spring day, not too cold or hot. It was sunny and the perfect day for a ride. Of course Jonah enjoyed riding no matter what the temperature was. Jeremiah appreciated riding as well, but more so when the weather was agreeable.

A moving truck was leaving the building when Jeremiah and Jonah arrived. It was on the way to Gabriel and Sarah's house for their upcoming move. As the team entered the warehouse, they were greeted by a clerk. The clerk looked over their requisitions for signatures, then handed the paperwork back to the partners.

"What are you looking for?" The clerk asked.

"A couple of motorcycles," Jeremiah replied.

"You will want the fourth floor. Another clerk will take your paperwork there." The clerk pointed to a big freight elevator to his left.

"Thanks," Jeremiah responded, as he looked around for Jonah. Jonah was sitting in an old muscle car. Jeremiah wondered how Jonah had gotten in there during Jeremiah's brief conversation with the clerk. It was an olive green 1968 Road Runner with the doors welded shut. Jonah had his hands on the wheel and was just grinning at Jeremiah.

"Jonah, come on! We need to go to the fourth floor to pick up the bikes."

"Okay, give me a second," Jonah replied.

Jeremiah glanced at the clerk for a mere second. He had a bewildered look on his face like someone with a case of indigestion. The clerk raised his eyebrows as he pointed to the car. When Jeremiah turned to see what was happening, he saw his friend's legs kicking about like scissors while attempting to dislodge his midriff from the window. It was like watching an overweight Santa Claus stuck in a chimney. Finally free from the car's grasp, Jonah pulled his shirt down that had wound up around his head. Out of breath and with a big smile on his face, Jonah exclaimed, "It was much easier getting in there than it was getting out."

The clerk shook his head at Jonah and Jeremiah as they headed for the elevator.

The basement of the warehouse held large means of transportation such as moving trucks, military vehicles, and boats. The first floor, as you already know, had vintage and sports cars. The second and third floors stored additional automobiles. The fourth floor supplied all types of motorcycles. The rest of the building was used to stock furniture, tools and all other equipment needed when working among the walking souls. After he had admired many motorcycles, Jonah settled on a turquoise and cream 1992 Harley Softail Classic. Jeremiah picked out a light green and white 2012 Indian Chief. Once the fourth floor clerk took the requisitions from the partners, they loaded the bikes onto the elevator and returned to the first floor. The two had decided to take Route 19, then Route 70 into Wheeling.

Jonah would have preferred to ride all back roads, but due to time restraints he would have to settle for a more direct route.

The moving truck backed up into the driveway, where Gabriel and Sarah had been living. Two men got out, greeted the team at the door and then got to work. A few neighbors peaked out of their windows to see the movers lugging furniture to the truck, then went back about their own business. The team would be renting a house on Duncan Avenue in the North Hills. There was an L.A. Fitness gym nearby. All of their future clients were members of the fitness center so it would give the team a chance to befriend them all in one place. Sarah had already made an appointment with a salesperson at the gym for the next morning. Gabriel was in the driveway and pretended to advise the movers when he saw another neighbor look out of their front window. He exchanged waves with the man, then went back inside. If an East End client stopped by for any reason after the team had moved, the neighbors would have let them know all about the moving truck. Nothing was out of the ordinary, and nothing was left to chance.

The failed attempt by the H.T. soldiers had all employees at the firm uneasy and on edge. Soahc had thrown fifteen soldiers into solitary confinement in the basement of the east coast office. Mehyam confined twenty-one military personnel on the west coast. As the prisoners were led through the dark hallway of the dungeon, others could be heard screaming for attention. Many of the prisoners hadn't had interaction with anyone in years and they were just hoping for a brief conversation with someone. The newly restrained soldiers tried to drag out the pace to their cell. They knew that before long they would be in the same shape as the prisoners that were begging them for a chat. Although they were tempted, not one of the soldiers acknowledged the prisoners for fear of adding time to their own sentences.

News of the freshly imprisoned soldiers had spread like wildfire throughout the H.T. employees. You would have thought it would put a damper on volunteers to take their place, but that wasn't the case. Most of them hated their jobs and jumped at the chance to do something else. Especially the workers who sat behind cramped desks, under bad lighting, and barely saw the outside world. The cell doors weren't even closed yet, but Covah and Lucifer were discussing the list of volunteers to replace the already forgotten combatants.

CHAPTER 10

The operative trio had arrived at a New York City satellite office. Because of the sensitive nature of their mission, only the office manager had been informed of their visit. He was a short, fast talking man who looked to be in his late fifties. His name was Noah. There were only a handful of employees in the office when the three co-workers arrived. Just so they didn't bring unwanted attention, Serafina and Michaela waited around the corner from the office, while Sephora entered the building. The office was located on Queens Boulevard, not far from the Queens Plaza subway stop. The structure was much smaller than the corporate offices in Pittsburgh and San Francisco, but larger than many other satellite offices. It was four stories high and, of course, not visible to walking souls.

Sephora entered the office building, walked up to the receptionist's desk and smiled, "Hello, my name is Sephora, I am here to see Noah. He should be expecting me."

"Good Afternoon. Just a moment please," the receptionist replied, as she picked up the phone and rang Noah's extension. After a brief conversation, the woman hung up, smiled and asked Sephora to have a seat and the manager would be right out. Before Sephora had time to pick up a magazine from the coffee table, Noah appeared. He was a little ball of energy, "Hello Sephora. I've been expecting you. Please follow me to my office." Noah walked quickly through the office. Sephora tried her best to keep up with him. When she reached his office, Noah looked both ways, then closed the door behind them.

"Are your teammates with you?" Noah asked inquisitively.

"Yes, but they are waiting around the corner. We thought it best if only one of us strolled into the office. To keep a low profile, you know?" Sephora smiled.

"Sure, I get it. Better safe than sorry" Noah replied, as he nervously jingled something in his pocket. Sephora turned her gaze toward his chiming pocket.

"Oh yes," Noah said, as he pulled the keys from his pants, "I have keys for your car. It's parked out back. Nothing fancy, it's a 2005 Cavalier, but it runs fine." Noah handed over the keys to Sephora. Before she had a chance to ask about the other keys on the ring Noah continued, "There are three copies of keys to your apartment also. We have a place near Flatbush Avenue on Chapel Street in Brooklyn. It is just a short drive across the Brooklyn Bridge and you will be at H.T. headquarters." Noah stopped for a second to catch his breath and to see if Sephora had any questions. Sephora smiled and nodded to him in agreement. With his mind catching up with his mouth, Noah piped up again as he pulled a piece of paper from his pocket, "Oh, I almost forgot. Here is the address of the apartment and also a few names of H.T. informants that we've used occasionally in the past. My direct line is on there as well."

Sephora stuffed the paper into her pocket and decided to read it later, outside. "Thank you for your help Noah," Sephora said as she stood up. "We will keep in touch." Noah nodded to Sephora, opened his office door and walked her back through the main office to the exit. Noah wished her luck as she left the building.

When Sephora returned to the corner to retrieve her coworkers, Serafina was sitting on a bench with her arms crossed, watching Michaela as she tormented a few walking souls that were jogging past them. Michaela was changing the songs on their iPods just to irritate them. Serafina raised her eyebrows at Michaela when she looked over. "What? Nobody talks to each other anymore?" Michaela asked.

As she approached her team, Sephora believed that they had made the right choice in having her, and not Michaela, meet with the office manager. Sephora filled the team in, as they walked around the back of the building. Serafina held out her hand and Sephora handed the car keys to her as usual. Serafina always drove the car.

Once Jeremiah and Jonah maneuvered their way out of the city traffic, they were enjoying the ride. The partners were taking in the scenery along the winding roads and Jonah was grinning like a teenager without a care in the world. He never turned down a chance to go on a road trip on a Harley. As the team merged onto Route 70, another group of bikes passed by. The two of them caught up and rode behind the group for the rest of the way to the Wheeling, West Virginia exit, where they split off from the other riders. The engines roared as the two rode through the tunnel and across the bridge before reaching Downtown Wheeling. Jeremiah and Jonah pulled into the parking garage at the Wheeling Majestic Casino and took the elevator upstairs where they had reserved a room at the casino hotel.

After checking in at the hotel, the team went to their room and dropped off their helmets and gear. The team checked in with the project leader on duty in Pittsburgh and notified the office of their arrival. The manager thanked the team for calling in and they agreed to be back in the office the following day. Jeremiah opened the curtains in the room and the partners stood at the window while they looked across the river at the ailing city. Jeremiah had always liked visiting Wheeling. As he scanned the town, he sighed, "It's a shame you know?" He paused for a moment, then continued, "I remember when this town was booming with business. Now they are struggling just to survive."

Jonah scanned the boarded up buildings as he patted his friend on the shoulder and said, "It certainly is a shame. The politicians have convinced the people that a casino would bring vitality to their city, but they don't realize it's the devil in a red dress." Jeremiah pulled the curtains closed and the two quietly left the room to go to work.

The team made their way through the casino floor between the walking souls. There were some happy faces in the crowd, but there was a higher percentage of less content people. Casinos were not in the business of losing money. Even when patrons had a lucky night, the house knew that they would get it back during the next visit. The dog track was situated outside, behind the casino. Jeremiah and Jonah took a seat behind an unshaven young man, who wore a baseball hat that advertised the casino name. The man was bouncing his knee and clinging to a ticket, as he anxiously awaited the next race. He paid no attention to the two when they took a seat behind him.

The trainers were parading the greyhounds along the track as they introduced the dogs to the betting audience. Jeremiah had started a conversation with Jonah, making sure that the young man could hear it clearly. "Jonah, you just got paid today. Are you sure you don't want to go to the grocery store first?"

"Not now Jeremiah, I can stop on the way home," Jonah grumbled.

"I think your wife and three kids might disagree. Is there any food in the house?" Jeremiah asked, as the trainers walked the dogs back to the gate.

"Of course there is. Don't lecture me," Jonah replied angrily.

"I am only trying to help Jonah. I know you are already behind on the rent and I don't want to see you and your family on the street. I am concerned for you buddy," Jeremiah said, just as the gates flew open and the dogs took off after the mechanical rabbit.

Jeremiah continued, "You know that your wife loves you, but how much do you think she is going to take before she decides that she's had enough?"

"Don't you worry about me buddy boy. I handle my own business," Jonah retorted. The young man had been looking at the floor during the conversation. He looked up in time to see his dog, Guilty Pleasure, cross the finish line in last place. The man dropped the ticket onto the floor as he stood up and shamefully left the dog track. He realized that the two men behind him had just described his life. He would stop for groceries on the way home, then apologize to his wife and family for neglecting his duties. On occasion it took a stranger to open one's eyes to a situation close to home.

On the way back through the casino, there was a man at the bar drinking a beer and using his best pick-up lines on a pretty young woman. Jonah walked up behind the man and asked, "Aren't you Joe Klein?"

The man looked at Jonah, confused. "Do I know you?" Joe asked apprehensively.

"I work at the mill too. Is this your wife?" Jonah asked, as he nodded to the woman who sat next to Joe.

"Uh, no, I just met her a few minutes ago," Joe replied, as the woman turned her attention elsewhere.

"Well, nice seeing you Joe," Jonah tapped the man on the back and walked away, without mention of his own name. The man was so upset that he put his beer on the bar and walked away without saying goodbye to the woman he had been trying so hard to impress. Jonah chuckled to himself, then turned to Jeremiah and said, "That ought to keep him worried and guessing for a while."

"And hopefully at home," Jeremiah replied.

The team had noticed some H.T. employees that tried not to be recognized as they walked around the casino floor. A few were at the poker tables wearing sunglasses, but were easily spotted by the two partners. Jonah nodded to one of the Broken as he passed by, but the H.T. worker pretended not to notice the gesture. Jeremiah and Jonah had a few more assignments that they had to deal with that evening before making their way back to their Pittsburgh office the next morning.

CHAPTER 11

The following morning, C.O.A. offices were back to a normal business day with the lack of military presence for the time being. Even though the militia had left the building, the employees were still on high alert status until further notice. Mark was in constant contact with General James and his colleagues in the west coast office. He had already briefed his department as well as the General, regarding the operatives that were set in place in New York City. The trio were expected to check in later in the day with an update on their status, unless something out of the ordinary occurred.

The movers had refurnished the new temporary home of Gabriel and Sarah in the North Hills. The laborers had moved their furniture so many times that they needed no direction from the tenants. When they had finished the night before, you would think that they had been living there for months. Everything was in place and there was no sign of boxes anywhere in the house. It was a similar layout of the house that the team had moved from, so the furniture fit perfectly.

Gabriel and Sarah were busy taking a tour of the L.A. Fitness with an eager salesperson, who gave a rehearsed speech and tried his best to sell a membership to the couple. The team listened attentively to the sales pitch, although it wasn't necessary, being that they had already planned to join the gym. It was the best place to have all of their new clients under one roof. In addition to many weight lifting and cardio exercise machines, there was a separate room for group exercise which included Pilates, Yoga, Aerobics and Spinning classes. The building also housed a pool, steam room, and sauna for relaxing after a hard workout. When the tour was over, the C.O.A. team paid their membership fee, which put another notch on the happy salesman's belt. They would return later in the afternoon to make contact with their new, unsuspecting clients.

New project managers were put in place for the day in the Pittsburgh office, and as usual, assignments were handed out during and after the 8:00 a.m. meeting. Most of the tasks were typical ones involving traffic or pedestrian incidents surrounding the morning rush. There were a few assignments dealing with domestic issues related to drugs and alcohol consumption that carried over from the night before.

There seemed to be somewhat more people involved in research within the Customer Relations Department, which came as no surprise. It had been made clear that Project Lost Faith would be a priority. Additional employees were looking into ways of reaching walking souls who had been lax or stagnant in their beliefs and revitalize their devotion. The personnel had to be creative in their pursuit of halfhearted followers and bring them back to their roots. C.O.A. employees knew that H.T. Enterprises would be trying to foil their plan at any cost, so they always needed to stay one step ahead of the competition.

Given the recent captivity of H.T. employees, the workforce had been on their best, or worst, behavior, depending on how you looked at it. None of them looked forward to joining the prisoners so they were willing to do whatever it took to stay out of the underground lodgings. Although the employee accommodations were nothing to get excited about, the basement cells were understood to be much worse. For workers that had not had the misfortune of spending time in solitary confinement, there was no shortage of tales depicting the experience.

When Soahc had personally ushered the last of the prisoners to his cell and locked the chamber, the inmate could hear the leader whistling a tune as he strolled down the hallway. It grew softer as he moved further away, until it was replaced by an extremely faint cry from another convict, who was housed too far away for conversation. It was so dark that the soldier had to feel his way around the room. As far as the inmate could tell, it was about five feet wide by five feet long. Not enough room to stretch out his whole body on the floor. There were, of course, no furnishings in the cell. The floor was damp and the only thing that shared the room with the detainee were the bugs and vermin crawling around. All he could do at that point was to hope for time to pass quickly.

On the other side of the East River from H.T. Enterprises, the three C.O.A. employees were already settled in at their temporary Brooklyn home. The modestly furnished apartment on Chapel Street was kept by C.O.A. as a safe house for operatives who were working in the area. It was close to H.T. headquarters, but far enough away to stay under the radar. While the H.T. prisoners were wishing they could get out, the trio was figuring out a way to get in, at least figuratively.

Sephora, Serafina and Michaela were sitting in the living room assessing the situation. Sephora placed the piece of paper, which Noah had given her at the office that morning, on the coffee table. Under Noah's phone number there were two names of informants. The first name was Repoh and the second was Rue. Those particular informants had been used in the past and were trusted sources for the C.O.A. Many H.T. moles had supplied minuscule accurate information at best, and many agents doubted if it was to be relied on at all. There were also informants that were willing to do whatever it took to get back into the good graces of C.O.A. Repoh and Rue had so far demonstrated to have been in the latter category, although the operatives would approach them with caution as always.

Sephora, who sat in a chair across the table from Michaela, tapped her finger on the note as she spoke up, "We need to take a ride and scope out the H.T. building."

"I agree, but not too close yet," Michaela replied.

"How will we recognize Repoh and Rue?" Serafina asked, as she looked through the curtains at the surrounding neighborhood.

"Noah has snapshots of them in a file locked in his office," Sephora replied.

"Couldn't he send the pictures over the phone?" Michaela asked.

"Too sensitive," Serafina said, while she watched two kids kick a can up the street.

"No electronic images exist of these two. They are much too important to the company," Sephora added. "We can meet Noah after we've done our initial surveillance."

The team left their apartment, walked to the back of the building and retrieved their blue Cavalier, parked in the alley. The car was nothing special, which was exactly what the ladies wanted. There were at least a thousand Chevy Cavaliers in the city with a similar paint color. Blending in with the walking souls was imperative to the mission. All three employees had turned off their glow lights before entering New York. Although they weren't followed, they didn't want to leave anything to chance. The team would not return to the New York office unless absolutely necessary. They would meet with Noah at different locations throughout the city. To preserve the idea of minimal electronic communication, the team would meet Noah at a donut shop on Flushing Avenue, at three o'clock. That was the last bit of information written on the note from Noah. All further meetings were to be prepared in advance. Serafina was behind the wheel of the car. Before she closed the driver's door, she burned the note and dropped the ash on the street.

The Marketing and Advertising Departments at C.O.A. were extraordinarily busy as they read through research material. It had been coming in faster than ever at the moment. The employees were preparing for an all employee meeting that was scheduled for later in the week. They wanted fresh ideas that would pump up the whole company. It would be a pep rally of sorts, and would emphasize the importance of Project Lost Faith. Electrifying the employees would be imperative to inspiring the minds of the walking souls. At the moment, the project was a high priority of the C.E.O. The marketing associates knew how significant the project was to their boss and they worked diligently to make it a success.

The west coast office was bustling as well. Their all employee meeting was scheduled for the day after the east coast office. The operatives in San Francisco were busy researching leads on their informants. They were whittling down the list to two or three of the most trustworthy of the Broken's confidants. They were given orders to postpone covert operations around the Hollywood H.T. building, for the time being. The New York team needed time to investigate and report back with their findings. It had been decided to send only one team at that time. If operative teams were exposed on both coasts simultaneously, H.T. Enterprises would assume high alert status. That action would set C.O.A. intelligence back weeks, if not months, and that was unacceptable. A lot was riding on the team in New York, and they were aware of their obligation.

CHAPTER 12

Jeremiah and Jonah had one stop on their ride home from Wheeling. It was in Claysville, PA. The team pulled into the Washington Hospital lot and parked their bikes. The two had been there before, and they knew their way around. They walked down the third floor hallway until they reached room 308. At the moment, the room was empty except for the patient in bed number one, Emma Baylor, and her guardian angel, Martha. Her family would be there shortly, but Emma was feeling nervous. Martha was standing behind Emma when Jeremiah and Jonah arrived. Emma saw the white glow of the team as they approached her. Martha also moved into Emma's view. Emma smiled at the three angels, then asked, "Have you come for me?"

"Not quite Emma. We are here to help with the anxiety," Jeremiah explained.

"I have always been with you Emma. I am your guardian angel, Martha," Martha revealed to Emma.

"Oh my goodness, you are so beautiful," Emma replied, putting her hand on Martha's, then continued, "I knew someone was watching over me." Emma was a strong believer, but the end of one's life can be a scary ordeal for the most stringent of believers.

"So you are not taking me?" Emma asked inquisitively.

"No, sweetheart," Jonah answered, "we are here to prepare you for your journey. Think of us as your travel guides."

"When the time comes, then who…" Emma paused for a moment, thinking to herself.

Martha squeezed Emma's hand, then said, "That's right Emma, the Lord will take you home."

Emma took a deep breath and peace enveloped her. She smiled at the angels and they sat quietly for a moment. Just then, a nurse entered the room to check on Emma. The nurse adjusted Emma's pillow, then began to take her blood pressure. Emma proudly announced to the nurse, "My guardian angel is here. Her name is Martha, and two of her friends are here also!" Jonah waved to the nurse, although he knew that she couldn't see him, but it amused Jeremiah just the same.

"Isn't that wonderful," the nurse replied, to appease Emma, as she watched the blood pressure gauge. "Your family is on the way Emma. They will be here soon." The nurse scurried out of the room to attend to another patient.

Gabriel had been attempting his first workout, in the weight room of the gym. Still gun-shy from his last encounter, he scanned the area and made sure that Seil was nowhere in sight. Gabriel was gratified for the moment that his nemesis was not in the gym. Three new clients had been working out together, not far from him. Gabriel stacked extra weight onto the bar, then attempted to bench press the weight. He made enough grunting noise to attract attention to himself. After lowering the weight bar to his chest, he flailed his legs, presumably struggling to lift the weight. He called out for help. The three men came to his rescue, effortlessly lifting the weights from Gabriel.

After they carefully secured the weight bar back to the bench, one of the men scolded Gabriel, "Whoa buddy, what were you thinking? You should never bench without a spotter."

"I thought I could handle it. Thanks for the help," Gabriel said as he pretended to catch his breath. "I am new to the gym and don't know anyone here. I will be more careful next time." Gabriel then introduced himself to the three men. They decided to take him under their wing and he finished the workout with his newfound friends. At the same time, Sarah had been taking an aerobics class with the wife and girlfriends of the three men. Everything had gone just as the team had planned.

When the aerobics class ended, Sarah met up with Gabriel in the steam room, where his new friends and their significant others had gathered. Gabriel introduced Sarah to his workout buddies and their companions.

The women acknowledged that they had seen Sarah in the class, but hadn't met her. During the steam and then a dip in the pool, the team spent some time getting acquainted with their latest apprentices.

***

New York traffic was atrocious as usual, especially on the Brooklyn Bridge. It would work to the advantage of Sephora and her coworkers. There would be less chance of being noticed among the other commuters. After she circled the block around H.T. headquarters, Serafina squeezed into a parking spot on Broad Street. The space was within eyesight of H.T. Enterprises' front door. Sephora and Michaela left the vehicle and walked into a drugstore while Serafina stayed in the car. As they browsed through items in the store, the two kept an eye on the building on Exchange Place. Within five minutes the team had picked up a few trinkets in the store, paid the clerk and returned to the Cavalier.

As the team drove away, they discussed their first look at the H.T. office. Although the visit was short, they were able to get a quick assessment. A few doors down from the drugstore was a coffee shop where people congregated to enjoy the complimentary Wi-Fi on their computers, as they consumed a snack and received their caffeine fix. The location of the coffee shop had a perfect view of H.T. Enterprises, and the team would utilize the hangout on their next surveillance. The ladies noticed a few guards pacing near the green slimy river surrounding the building, but the moat door was closed. During their short observation, no one had left or entered the gloomy structure. With the sealed appearance of the office, it was clear that it was not business as usual.

Jeremiah, Jonah and Martha stayed with Emma Baylor while she said goodbye to her loved ones. Her anxiety had passed once she realized she would not be alone on her journey and she went peacefully. With many walking souls, there were two things that worried them most when leaving this world. One was leaving their families and friends. The other was a fear of the unknown. The angels helped to ease their crossing and calm their nerves.

Upon their departure from Washington Hospital, Jeremiah and Jonah resumed their scenic ride back to Pittsburgh. Jonah led the way, taking the longest route possible. He was trying to delay the inevitable. He hated to return the motorcycle, but it was time to get back to work. As the team pulled up to the warehouse, Jonah assumed his usual forlorn expression—that of a kid who has dropped his ice cream in a mud puddle. The team turned in the bikes, along with the R.A. paperwork to the clerk. Before Jonah had taken two steps toward the race car in the lobby, Jeremiah shouted sternly, "Jonah!" Jonah's smile turned to a pout as he lowered his head, crossed his arms and followed behind Jeremiah without a word.

New recruits were brought in for orientation once a month at C.O.A. Once the angels had time to acclimate to their new world, they would be offered positions with C.O.A. The Angel Resources Director was currently speaking to new hires in the auditorium, on the ninety-ninth floor in Pittsburgh. It had been a good month for C.O.A. Approximately one thousand new employees would join the company on the east coast. The eager trainees listened carefully as the director went over the duties of their new careers. Working at C.O.A. was considered to be a great honor. It was a position that was desired by many, but offered to a small percentage.

The Assistant Director was handing out assignments to the fresh workforce. Some would be assigned to the corporate office. Most of them would be assigned to satellite offices, located somewhere on the east coast. They would begin training the next day. Each one of the new recruits would be assigned to a mentor team that would show them the ropes for the next few months. Although each circumstance was different, most employees had a three month probationary period. If all went well, after the trial period the trainee would be paired with a seasoned partner.

While the Assistant Director finished passing out paperwork to the employees regarding their relocation, the Director continued talking to the workforce. As she paced back and forth in front of the audience, she explained that an employee could request a transfer after one year, but the initial placement was non-negotiable. After one year, an employee could request to be placed in the same state where they grew up, but not in the same city. Employees were able to inquire about family and friends from their former life, but contact was strictly prohibited and grounds for dismissal. The company didn't want the employees involved in situations that would bring personal feelings into the mix. Working with walking souls in which the employee had a relationship could cause complications. For that reason, workers were initially assigned to offices far from their hometowns. In the event that someone from their past life became part of an assignment, the employee was required to contact the project leader immediately. The manager would then transfer the assignment to another team.

When the A.R. Director finished her speech, she took a few questions from the crowd. After all inquiries were answered and she felt confident that the recruits understood what was expected of them, they were dismissed from the meeting. They would be expected on the job the next morning at their respective locations for the eight a.m. meetings.

CHAPTER 13

Serafina found a parking spot across the street from the donut shop on Flushing Avenue. She glanced at her watch: it was 2:50 p.m. Michaela noticed a man in black rimmed glasses sitting at a table by himself. He stopped tapping his fingers on the table only long enough to check the time on his watch.

"Is that him?" Michaela inquired hesitantly.

"Yes," Sephora responded. "He's anxious enough Michaela. Don't egg him on."

"Got it," Michaela replied respectfully as the trio filed out of the car.

Noah recognized Sephora as she entered the shop and they nodded to each other. The girls ordered a coffee, then joined Noah at his table. He was introduced to the other members of the team. Noah resumed tapping on a folder that sat in front of him, on the table.

"Did you bring the photos Noah?" Sephora asked as she motioned to the folder.

"Yes, here they are," Noah replied, pushing the folder to Sephora as he scanned the room for prying eyes.

She carefully slid the photographs out of the folder.

"This is Repoh," Noah said, pointing to the picture, as the team studied the face. He was clean cut, average height, with sandy brown hair. He looked to be in his late-twenties. He was younger and better looking than the team had imagined. Sephora pulled the 2nd photo out and slipped it on top of the other. "This is Rue," Noah informed the team, then began to tap his foot on the wooden floor.

Michaela grimaced at Noah, then pushed her hand down onto Noah's knee to suppress the annoying noise. He gave her half a smile as he tried to sit still.

Rue looked to be in his mid-twenties with shoulder length dark brown hair. He was more unkempt than Repoh. His face was unshaven and his hair looked like he had just rolled out of bed. Both of them had similar thin builds, but with distinct characteristics. Sephora glanced at her teammates with raised eyebrows. Serafina and Michaela both nodded in acknowledgement that they had memorized the faces. Sephora returned the photos back to the folder, then slid it across the table to Noah.

Noah told the operatives that the best place to make contact with Repoh would be on the subway. "He spends a lot of time between lower Manhattan and the Flatiron District. He has descriptions of you three, and is anticipating your meeting. Rue often works near Central Park. He is expecting you as well. Let's meet here tomorrow at 6:00 p.m." Noah picked up the folder and stood up to leave. The girls agreed with the plan, and waited for Noah to leave the establishment, then returned to their car.

Mark received a call from the team in New York. The conversation was short and sweet. He relayed the information on to his department and his west coast colleagues. Although there wasn't much to report for the moment, he wanted to keep all concerned parties updated. He promised additional reports as facts became available. In the meantime, both offices would keep up with their own online research.

Gabriel was at the new house on Duncan Avenue, recuperating from his earlier work out when he received an unexpected call from Josh Alexander, one of his East End clients. The man had joined a church in the area and wanted to share his news with Gabriel. As the two talked, Josh expressed interest in starting a group for people his age to get together and discuss their views on religion. Josh wanted to run it by Gabriel to see what he thought about it. Gabriel was excited to hear Josh taking such an interest, but also a little surprised. Josh was fairly quiet and a little backward. Gabriel remembered the advice that his supervisor had given earlier. He tried to keep an open mind and offered to help. The two of them talked for a long time. Josh mentioned that the pastor of his church was more than happy to let the group meet in their conference room. Gabriel said it would be his pleasure to help distribute flyers for Josh's meetings.

Gabriel and Sarah reported the conversation back to the project managers in the Marketing Department. They were happy to hear about a new prospect working with the team and they agreed to help in any way possible to keep the momentum going. His supervisor said that it would be a great benefit to the neighborhood and hopefully the city. He also reminded Gabriel to look past the small things and keep an eye on the big picture. Gabriel understood. He promised to mentor Josh and point him in the right direction. If all went well, when the time was right, Gabriel and Sarah would casually inform their new clients about the upcoming meetings.

After the A.R. Director dismissed the new recruits from the conference room, employees in the Marketing Department took over the room to hang some banners and began to decorate for the upcoming all employee meeting. Although they had plenty of time, the team wanted to be proactive. Some of the new recruits had volunteered to stay and help the department.

Many of the new recruits had decided to hang out for a while at the C.O.A. building, since they weren't needed to be on site until the following morning. They visited different departments to get a feel for how things operated at headquarters. Jonah figured since he was in between assignments at the moment, he would use the time to annoy some of the new employees. He remembered how intimidating his first day on the job had been, so he decided not to be too hard on them. They were like freshmen on the first day of high school. Eager to fit in, but not knowing what to expect. Although Jonah didn't know it at the time, most of the recruits had already been warned about the prankster at orientation.

The project manager on duty had noticed Jonah's boredom and rewarded the team with a new assignment. It was better for all concerned to keep Jonah occupied. The team had been dispatched to traffic duty on Centre Avenue, in Shadyside. Jonah loved it. He wore a policeman's uniform and had a whistle, which Jeremiah thought he enjoyed a little too much. As Jeremiah repaired a cracked manhole on the road, Jonah maneuvered the traffic onto Baum Blvd. Jeremiah chuckled to himself as he watched Jonah with his hand motions and whistle. It didn't take much to amuse Jonah, Jeremiah thought to himself while he continued repairs of the manhole cover.

Covah had passed on orders to Mehyam and Soahc to resume normal operations, which meant business as usual in the field. They were at least to give the appearance that things were back to normal. H.T. presumed that

C.O.A. had noticed their buildings closed up and people being reined in. H.T. thought it would cause less suspicion if they loosened the reins a little. That was good news for Repoh and Rue. With restrictions being lifted, it would be easier to make contact with Sephora and her team. They needed to take every precaution while on the outside. Getting caught would be disastrous, not only to the informants, but also to the C.O.A. operation.

Serafina and the team drove around the block of H.T. headquarters to get another look. They noticed that the front door had been once again opened. Like Repoh and Rue, the team was pleased to see that. Two guards were still parading outside of the building, but during the team's surveillance they saw traffic moving in and out of the building. It was seven o'clock at the time. They agreed to return to the apartment until nightfall, then hop on the subway and hopefully meet up with Repoh.

Mehyam and Soahc had also been informed by Covah that there would be an upcoming meeting to discuss new business at H.T. Enterprises. They were not privy to the time or place of the next meeting. They would be contacted in the near future. The leaders were not to tell anyone else about the impending consultation. They were also advised to keep an eye on their people. Mehyam and Soahc had instructed their supervisors to advise them of any unusual C.O.A. activity in the area. The leaders were to report anything out of the ordinary to Covah immediately, given the fact that restrictions had been lifted among the employees.

The news had spread quickly throughout C.O.A. Mark had been informed about the recent constraints being relaxed. The company would show a presence in both cities as usual, but not an overwhelming presence. Like H.T. Enterprises, they also wanted to show the appearance of business as usual, especially in New York. They wanted the Broken to see typical movement and nothing odd that could blow the cover of the concealed operatives.

CHAPTER 14

Covah and Soahc were having a discrete meeting in Soahc's office. The room was small in comparison to other offices, but private. There were no windows, besides the glass in the top half of the door, in which the blind was drawn. The two were having a conversation with someone on a speaker phone and they had the volume down low enough that no one outside of the office could hear their conversation. Following with the décor of the rest of H.T. headquarters, Soahc's office was damp and musty. The light on the ceiling buzzed lightly and dimmed in and out, like that of a tired heartbeat. The floor outside of the office creaked with the slightest of weight applied to it, which was no coincidence. If even a mouse scampered by, the two would hear it.

Once Covah and Soahc had finished their brief call, they pulled their chairs closer together.

Covah whispered to Soahc, "I want everyone to believe that we are under normal conditions on the shop floor."

"I understand," Soahc said as he nodded.

"If we have anyone that is not doing as they are told, He will flush them out," Covah continued as he stood up to leave the office, "and we will show no mercy."

Soahc forced a smile, then nodded again to Covah, as he opened the door and left the office. Soahc sat quietly for a moment while Covah's footsteps grew fainter as he made his way down the hallway. He was on his way to tell Lucifer that their plan was in motion.

Sephora, Serafina and Michaela were back at the apartment in Brooklyn, for the moment. Sephora and Serafina sat quietly on the couch and briefly enjoyed some peace. Michaela had a hard time sitting still. She continually paced around the room and glanced out of the window. Her restlessness was getting on Serefina's last nerve.

"Will you sit down already?" Serefina said with raised eyebrows.

"I can't help it. How long are we going to sit around here waiting?" Michaela responded, impatiently.

Serefina tapped Sephora on her elbow and laughed, "Who does she remind you of?"

"Noah," both women spouted out, with a giggle.

"Very funny!" Michaela smirked at the two of them as she plopped herself onto the chair.

They would hold off a little longer before spending the rest of the evening on the subway.

Hopefully the trio would be able to see Repoh.

C.O.A. Pittsburgh had been pretty quiet for a change as well. Like Michaela, that didn't sit well with Jonah either. It was easier for Jeremiah to keep Jonah out of trouble when he was busy. Jeremiah enjoyed the downtime once in a while. He was seated on an easy chair relishing a few minutes of silence, when he heard a small commotion down the hall. Jeremiah rolled his eyes as he peeled himself from the chair.

"No rest for the weary," he thought to himself as he left to see what Jonah was up to.

There were still some new recruits hanging around the office, before having to leave for their assigned posts. When Jeremiah rounded the corner, he saw Jonah laying on the floor covered from head to toe in Silly String. There were three new recruits standing over him, with their arms raised in victory. When the new employees noticed Jeremiah, they hid the cans behind their backs, but looked guilty. Jonah flashed Jeremiah an impish grin as he laid on the floor.

"How old are you?" Jeremiah scolded Jonah.

Jonah paused and looked to the ceiling as he counted on his fingers. "Two hundred and fifty two, this past March," Jonah replied proudly.

The new recruits busted out laughing along with Jonah.

"Well act your age," Jeremiah tried to hold back a smile. "Let's see if we can find something constructive for you to do." Jeremiah shooed away the new recruits, as Jonah brushed himself off and followed Jeremiah to see if the project leader could find the team some busy work.

Gabriel and Sarah had spent much of the evening calling on past acquaintances to inform them of Josh Alexander's discussion group that would meet the next day, at East Side Baptist Church. Many of their friends promised to attend the discussion and the team would be there as well. They had posted plenty of flyers in the area and expected a good turnout for the meeting. Gabriel had invited the team's gym buddies also. They promised to try and make it there too.

Mark was sitting at his desk on the ninetieth floor. Something had been bothering him as he stared at his computer. He couldn't explain the feeling. He had heard from the team in New York that the Broken had resumed business as usual, but something didn't seem right to Mark. Call it a hunch, but he would take all precautions to watch for anything out of the ordinary. Everyone in the department was busy collecting data and watching security footage from cameras, which had been placed strategically outside H.T. headquarters and the near vicinity of the building in New York. Even when the rest of the corporation had a lull in the excitement, the Intelligence Department was busy checking and re-checking their data for the slightest discrepancy. One of the employees had called Mark over to show him a peculiar video feed from H.T. Mark leaned over the man's shoulder and focused on the computer screen. The footage had been rewound and paused.

"Go ahead," Mark said, as the man resumed the video.

"Do you see these three people coming out right here?" The man pointed to his monitor.

"Yes, but I can't see their faces," Mark squinted.

"Exactly. They are covered from head to toe in black clothing, and they seem to be trying to avoid being detected. I almost missed them, they were moving so fast," the man said.

Mark kept his eye on the video, but the three figures disappeared in an instant.

"Good work. Let me know if you see anything else," Mark patted the guy on the shoulder, then went back to his desk. He rubbed his chin while he sat in silence for a few seconds. "What are you up to H.T.?" he thought to himself. His hunch was right, but he had to find out who those figures were, and what were they planning? Mark picked up the phone and talked to his west coast counterpart to inform him of the latest findings and make sure they watched out for any unusual activity near H.T. Hollywood. Mark hung up the phone after a brief conversation. He glanced at his watch. He expected the operatives in New York to call him in a few hours with an update. In the meantime, he would keep an eye on the camera recordings.

Serafina found a parking space on the street, near the Penn Station entrance, on West 32nd Street. That was a miracle in itself, to find a space on the street so late at night. Most of the spots were usually taken by that time. Before the trio had left the car, Sephora reminded the other two of Repoh's description: "He is clean cut and average height, with sandy brown hair. A good-looking kid in his late-twenties. Got it?"

Serafina and Michaela both nodded in agreement.

"We will split up once we get on the subway. If either of you see Repoh, text me. I will see if it's safe to make contact with him. Any questions?" Sephora asked.

"We understand," Serafina replied. "Got it," Michaela answered.

There were more people than you would think riding the subway at two in the morning. Most of the passengers were making their way home from the bar. By two-thirty a.m. the crowd had thinned out immensely. The women had been on the train for three hours by then, but there was no sign of Repoh so far. The threesome hadn't switched trains in an hour or so. They had decided to get off at Times Square, then board the next train on the route. Like clockwork, another one had pulled up to board passengers about two minutes later.

When the girls entered the car, Serafina had found an empty seat next to an older woman. Michaela turned left and went to the next car. Sephora moved to a car to the right of where they had boarded. As Sephora took a seat, she noticed that there were only five people in the car. She soon realized why. The whole car smelled of B.O. and alcohol. Two passengers were drunken college buddies who were being a little loud and obnoxious, but harmless. Another was a homeless man whose head bounced against the window, while he slept. Then Sephora saw Repoh, seated a few seats down from the homeless man. A quick glance at him, then she fiddled with something in her purse and settled back in her seat. When she looked at

Repoh again, he cautiously motioned his eyes to the left, then coolly looked out of the window on his right side.

Sephora waited a few seconds, then she glanced further back on the train car. She saw a man holding up a newspaper, which obstructed the view of his face.

Sephora's phone rang. It was Serafina. Sephora pretended to be talking to her mother. She said that she was almost home and would be getting off of the train at the next stop. Serafina relayed the coded message to Michaela. Sephora continued a phony conversation with herself as she waited for the mystery man to lower the newspaper. When he did, Sephora diligently snapped his picture with her phone. When the train came to a stop at the next station, Sephora stood up, careful not to acknowledge Repoh in any way, and all three women exited their separate cars.

CHAPTER 15

Mark's concern in Pittsburgh prompted the San Francisco office to work through the night monitoring security feeds at HT Hollywood. The Broken came and went from the building in small clusters, which was not abnormal. Right before dawn, a group of employees left the structure, with about ten to twelve people huddling closely.

After reaching the end of the moat, two figures split from the group to the left, as the others continued on before dispersing. The team rewound the tape and played it back in slow motion. As was the case in New York, they were unable to see the faces of the two Broken that had split from the group before they disappeared into what was left of the darkness.

Business was booming bright and early the next morning at C.O.A. The eight a.m. meeting began with new project leaders handing out assignments and the worker bees were heading out of the office to various parts of the city. There were traffic problems and tempers flared, due to a hard spring rain that mucked up the early morning commute. The downpour led to flooding issues throughout the city as well. Employees were sent to work on water mains and clogged sewers, which could impact major routes in and out of the city. Some workers were dispersed to keep an eye on the lock & dams on the Allegheny River, to make sure they were functioning correctly.

The ninety-ninth floor had been bustling as well. Some of the new hires had stayed to decorate the conference room for the upcoming employee meeting. The last of them left early in the morning to report to their assigned positions. The ladies in A.R., along with a few other employees, were busy putting the finishing touches on the room. They were glad to have had the help from the recruits and seemed very happy with the results.

Mark and his team on the ninetieth floor were still collecting data on their computers and meticulously scanning video from New York. No one had spotted the mystery men since they first appeared the night before. Mark had received a phone call from San Francisco, before the eight a.m. meetings. There had been no further sightings of the two unidentified figures at H.T. Hollywood. Both men promised to contact one another with any news.

Sephora had called Noah as soon as the women returned to the apartment, late the night before, to set up an early morning meeting. No details had been discussed over the phone. New York City traffic was atrocious as usual. Serafina circled the block for a parking space near the donut shop on Flushing Avenue. After having no luck, she dropped off Sephora and Michaela a few doors away before repeating the process. The girls didn't want to keep Noah waiting.

Sephora and Michaela ordered a coffee at the counter. The shop was crowded with walking souls rushing to get that last cup of coffee before heading to work. Sephora noticed Noah at a corner table. As usual, he was nervously tapping his fingers on the table and glancing at his watch. When Noah spotted Sephora in line, he seemed to calm down a bit. The girls exchanged greetings with Noah as they sat down. Sephora told Noah that Serafina would be along as soon as she found a parking space. Michaela frowned at Noah as he started with his bouncing knee. He was so fidgety.

"I didn't think I would see you until this afternoon," Noah started. "What happened?"

"We saw Repoh on the subway last night," Sephora replied.

"That's good news," Noah appeared enthusiastic.

"Not really," Michaela chimed in.

Sephora pulled her phone from her purse and scanned the coffee shop for peering eyes before holding up the picture of the mystery man on the subway. Noah turned white as a ghost when he saw the man. His jaw dropped, and for the moment he sat extremely still. Michaela thought he was having a stroke. Sephora laid the phone face down on the table. Michaela put her hand on top of Noah's. "Hey, are you alright?"

The color slowly returned back to Noah's face and then he looked flushed, "Nobody has seen him in years. We weren't sure he was still in the area. We've only ever seen sketches of him. As far as I know, this is the first picture I've ever seen of him!"

Sephora and Michaela were on the edge of their seat, when Serafina approached the table and startled the others, "Whoa, it's just me," Serafina said, with raised hands, as she slid into a chair.

"Who is he?" Sephora asked, once regaining her composure.

Noah leaned in and whispered, "His name is Degarne." Noah seemed to forget about his nervous tick as he stared blankly at the table, which made Michaela nervous. "Noah!" she exclaimed, poking his arm to jerk him back to reality.

"Degarne is considered to be the fiercest of the Broken's army," Noah blurted out, "Some think he is only a myth, but we know better. He is said to be so ruthless that even Lucifer has trouble controlling him!"

"Was he looking for us, or following Repoh?" Serafina piped up.

"I'm not sure," Noah replied. "I would like to take your phone back to the office with me Sephora. I want to download his picture on a secure line and put it in the vault." Sephora slid her phone to Noah, he put it in his pocket and said, "I will clean it and get it back to you later today. I will also contact Mark, to bring him up to speed." Sephora nodded to Noah in agreement.

"Let's meet at five p.m. There is a Starbucks on 3rd Avenue, in the East Village. Hopefully I will have more answers for you then. We've been here twice, at the donut shop. I don't want to raise suspicion," Noah said softly, when he stood up to leave.

Much to everyone's surprise in Pittsburgh, one of the new recruits that had been involved in the silly string incident was assigned to Jeremiah and Jonah. Jonah was as excited as a new father, while Jeremiah was not as thrilled. He had his hands full with Jonah, not to mention an easily swayed newbie as well. The newbie's name was Theo. The team had requisitioned a river boat from the warehouse in the Strip District. Surprisingly Jeremiah was able to keep Jonah away from Primanti's, and the race cars during the ordeal. Jeremiah wondered if Jonah was turning over a new leaf? Not a chance, he decided.

As the partners slid the boat into the water, Theo hopped aboard and asked, "Can I drive?"

"No!" Jeremiah and Jonah resounded in unison. Theo sat down, crossed his arms and pouted.

Jeremiah tapped Jonah on the shoulder. "Remind you of anyone?" "No one comes to mind," Jonah said sarcastically, with a puckish grin. New hires' wings were not fully developed. They had two sets of wings that would become fuller with time and experience. The feathers of a new hire's wings were short and sparse, and not as white as a seasoned angel. The new hires were easily spotted. Not only by C.O.A., but the Broken as well. For that reason, the new employees were expected to shadow their mentor at all times so that they were not confronted by the opposition. Besides their physical appearance, they seemed like awkward teenagers. They were full of energy and inquisitiveness. Something that Jonah never quite seemed to have outgrown. The corporation thought it may be good for Jonah to take on that new responsibility. Jeremiah and Jonah boarded the boat and Jonah jumped to the controls. "Untie us from the dock Newbie." Jonah spouted, "All hands on deck!" Jonah shifted into reverse, as Jeremiah took a seat next to Theo, who gathered up the rope.

The A.R. Director was satisfied with the conference room decorations on the ninety-ninth floor. She sat quietly at her desk and enjoyed a little downtime. She smiled to herself as she wondered how Jonah was making out with his new protégé. Not to worry, she would find out soon enough. No news was good news, she thought, as she opened one of the many folders piling up on her desk.

Gabriel and Sarah had a morning workout at the gym with their new friends. They reassured the team that they would see them later in the afternoon at the East Side Baptist Church. With a quick phone call to Josh Alexander, Gabriel calmed Josh's nerves and gave him some encouragement for the upcoming meeting. Although Gabriel still had his doubts, he assured Josh that everything would be fine. He told Josh that he and Sarah looked forward to the meeting.

The new information relayed to the west coast office regarding Degarne was the break they needed to move forward. Hollywood H.T. had used an operative called Regna, for special occasions. Although he wasn't as aloof as Degarne, he was considered to be almost as treacherous. The west coast office hadn't seen Regna for close to a year, but they had a surveillance picture of him. Thomas, who was the head of intelligence in San Francisco, printed out a picture of Regna, to be distributed on each floor of the building.

Thomas thought to himself, "Of course. It has to be Regna. How could I have missed it?"

Thomas forwarded Regna's picture to Mark in Pittsburgh to keep him in the loop, then sat back, closed his eyes and tried to predict Regna's next move.

CHAPTER 16

Gabriel and Sarah had arrived by 3:45 p.m. at the East Side Baptist Church. They found Josh Alexander reviewing his notes and nervously talking to himself in a church pew. Gabriel patted Josh on the shoulder with encouragement, "Sounds good Josh. Don't worry. You got this."

"I hope so," Josh replied. "There are already fifteen people here. I told them to make themselves comfortable, have a soft drink and I would be right back. I am not so good in front of a big group."

Sarah rubbed his shoulder, then a calm came over Josh, "You're going to do great. Come on, we will walk in with you."

Five more people showed up before four o'clock. It wasn't a bad turnout for the first meeting, especially considering the weather. Josh stood up and cheerfully introduced himself with new found confidence. A little gift from Sarah. Everyone really enjoyed the informal discussion and looked forward to meeting again. Gabriel and Sarah were full of hope and pleased to see their efforts were working within the walking souls. Since the meeting had gone so well, another one was scheduled for the next evening.

Seil, who had been watching through the window from outside, decided not to formally attend the meeting that night. He crumpled up the flyer in his hand, then changed his mind. He smoothed out the paper again, then stuffed it into his pocket, before he left. John Alexander looked to be an easy target, from Seil's perspective.

Back in New York, Serafina had found a parking space on the first try near the Starbucks on 3rd Avenue, which tickled her. The girls arrived before Noah for a change, so they picked a table near the back wall. Sephora couldn't forget the evil she saw in Degarne's face. His red eyes looked like they could burn a hole right through you. He had slicked back coal black hair and a Fu Manchu mustache, as if he wasn't scary looking enough. Sephora was glad that Repoh had warned her before she made contact with him. She went over the incident in her mind and decided that Degarne hadn't realized who she was. But now that he had seen her, she would need to be very vigilant.

Noah had arrived five minutes early. He checked his watch as he ordered a cappuccino. He was pleased to see the team was already in attendance. Michaela was happy too. She figured it might curb Noah's anxiety a bit. "What's up Noah?" Michaela asked, putting her hand up for a high five.

"Uh, not much?" Noah raised his hand in what looked more like a Vulcan greeting. He was not much for small talk. The gesture made Michaela laugh, while Noah just looked puzzled. The whole situation annoyed Serafina, as she curled her lip and scolded Michaela, "Knock it off!"

"Okay, that's enough," Sephora said calmly. "What did you find out Noah?"

"Right, Degarne. As far as we could tell, he is sniffing out any problems within the ranks. After the last fiasco, H.T. headquarters did not want any more surprises. We think it is just a coincidence that he was watching Repoh, but we aren't positive."

"Yes, and he's seen my face now," Sephora replied.

"That's why I think we need to take it slow for now," Noah said, "we will keep an eye out for Degarne, but we will watch Repoh the next few days, to make sure Degarne isn't on his tail. Once we are satisfied, then you can try once again to make contact with Repoh. If my intuition is correct, Degarne will shadow Rue as well in the near future. Let's hold off looking for him for now." Noah slid Sephora's scrubbed phone to her across the table. "Let's meet here again tomorrow, same time." The girls agreed, then left Noah to his cappuccino.

In Pittsburgh, the flooding had subsided for the most part. The rivers and creeks were still high, but manageable. All of the locks & dams were operational. They were holding back or releasing water, as they should have been. Many employees were still out helping with cleanup efforts, but it wasn't as hectic as it had been earlier in the day. The best part was that there had been no fatalities due to the inclement weather.

Any day that involved a motorcycle, boat or race car, was a great day for Jonah. Their mission on the river had been a success and everyone was safe. The team returned the boat in one piece, which made the warehouse content. Jonah was so busy sharing stories with the newbie that he didn't pout once as they returned the boat, which impressed Jeremiah. Maybe the intern would be a good thing. Time would tell, Jeremiah thought as he watched Jonah walk with his arm around Theo's shoulder.

Later that evening, it seemed to be a quiet night in Pittsburgh. After the flooding had subsided, most walking souls were just happy to be home and able to relax, before doing it all again the next day. Not many people were on the road, so it was a quiet night for C.O.A. as well. Many of the angels used their downtime to catch up on the day's paperwork. Jeremiah listened to Jonah telling Theo some of his war stories, while Theo intently soaked it all in. Jeremiah smiled, knowing that Jonah was in his glory.

Mark and his people were busy scanning all of the New York subway footage for traces of Degarne. Noah had sent a photo by messenger to Mark, so that they could recognize Degarne. C.O.A. didn't want any electronic pictures out there that could be noticed by the Broken. So far Mark's team had not seen any trace of Degarne, although copies of his picture were hanging all over the department. It was imperative that all employees recognized his face. The safety of the team in New York depended on it.

Gabriel and Sarah had met with their supervisor, Benjamin, to let him know about Josh Alexander's meeting at the East Side Baptist Church. The supervisor was very pleased with the success of the meeting and urged the team to keep Josh optimistic in his chairing of the group gatherings. Gabriel and Sarah promised to keep Josh upbeat, knowing that it was beneficial to them as well. Sarah also explained how she had helped Josh with his self-confidence, so that he could overcome the shyness he struggled with. She assured Benjamin that after a few more meetings, he would be leading the group like a pro. The team would meet up with their new clients at the gym the next day to find out how they were progressing. The supervisor was satisfied with the headway that Gabriel and Sarah had made. He told them that their achievements would be brought up at the upcoming employee meeting, which pleased the team. Sarah and Gabriel said goodnight to Benjamin, then headed back to their home in the North Hills for the evening.

Sephora, Serafina and Michaela had decided to stay off of the subway for the night. They took a ride in the car past H.T. headquarters, just to get a feel for anything out of place. On the outside, everything looked normal. There was a guard patrolling and the moat was down, which gave the impression of an ordinary evening at H.T. The girls made a few passes around the block and saw employees coming and going from the structure, which was normal operating procedure for the Broken. During the last pass, they saw the sentinel throw some food scraps to the creatures in the nasty green goo under the moat. He seemed to get a kick out of watching the monsters snapping at each other as they fought for the scraps. The trio decided to return to the apartment in Brooklyn and hang low for the evening.

Inside the H.T. building, had been anything but calm. The Broken knew that Degarne was on the prowl and they didn't want their name to come up in conversation with Covah or Soahc. At that moment, Degarne was in a closed meeting with the two leaders along with Lucifer, in his office. The rest of the employees kept their heads down, as they tried to keep busy and out of sight. There was not much chatter going on at H.T. Anyone who felt the urge to speak, made sure they did so quietly, for the time being. It was so quiet during Lucifer's meeting that the annoying humming from the lights seemed to echo more than ever. Aside from the buzzing, the only other sounds came from the dungeon. The cries and screams of the prisoners could be heard through the vents. That noise was no coincidence. Covah and Soahc had purposely funneled the cries throughout the building. It served as a reminder to the rest of the employees that they did not want to end up restrained like their coworkers.

Repoh had been riding the subway on his usual route in lower Manhattan. He knew that he wouldn't see Sephora and her team for a few days. He would go about his normal workday and wait until it was safe for the two of them to speak. Repoh had hoped to run into Rue during his time on the train. He knew it was much too dangerous for them to have a conversation within the building. Repoh wanted to make sure Rue knew that Degarne had been lurking about. He didn't want Rue to be noticed talking to the C.O.A. operatives either. Getting out of the H.T. building was the only thing that kept Repoh sane. Most people wouldn't consider riding the subway all night a treat, but to Repoh it was one of the best positions within the company. Repoh was not easily rattled, which made him the perfect informant for the

C.O.A. He knew that Degarne was shadowing him, but he kept his cool. His level headed demeanor kept him out of the limelight, and that was exactly what Repoh wanted. Degarne seemed satisfied that Repoh didn't notice he had been tailed, so he moved onto another worker. Repoh was a little concerned about Rue. He was careful for the most part, but unlike Repoh, Rue didn't have as good a poker face. Repoh decided that he would ride past Central Park, to see if he might bump into Rue. He would feel much better about the situation if they could make contact soon.

CHAPTER 17

Early the next morning, Mark had received a phone call from Thomas at the San Francisco office. His intuition was correct. Thomas and his team had noticed Regna on surveillance video, near H.T. Hollywood. They would continue to monitor Regna's movements, but Thomas presumed that Regna was looking for problem employees, as was the east coast office. There was one question that Mark and Thomas both had wondered. What had prompted the operation? Was someone at H.T. tipped off, or was it just paranoia setting in? Mark and Thomas promised to keep in touch before they hung up.

Gabriel and Sarah were up bright and early and off to the gym. A few of their new clients had been getting in a quick workout before heading into work for the day. The team was anxious to see how they felt about Josh's get-together. One of the couples were on the treadmill when Gabriel and Sarah walked in. "Speak of the devil," the man said, smiling at the team. Gabriel hated that expression, but returned the smile.

"We were just saying how much we enjoyed last night," the man continued. "We are all looking forward to next week."

"Excellent!" Gabriel replied, "We thought you would enjoy it. As a matter of fact, with the success from last night, another meeting has been added for this evening."

Sarah chimed in, "Josh is a great guy, and easy to talk to." Gabriel and Sarah were happy with the progress they were making with the new clients.

The 8 a.m. meeting had been getting ready to start at C.O.A. Jeremiah and Jonah were the project leaders on the second floor that morning.

Jeremiah wore a dark suit and tie, with a white shirt. That was how he was most comfortable. To his right was Jonah. Jonah wore his biker vest as usual, but instead of a T-shirt, he also wore a white dress shirt along with a black tie that portrayed a Harley emblem. Jeremiah watched Jonah tug at his collar. Jonah hated wearing ties, but had been trying his best to look professional. Jeremiah squinted at Jonah for a second, which caught Jonah's eye. "What's the matter?" Jonah asked.

"Is that mousse in your beard?" Jeremiah chuckled.

"Why yes, it is," Jonah stroked his chin. "I even used a conditioner, to make it more manageable," he said proudly, as he looked to Theo for approval, who was seated in the front row. Theo gave Jonah a big grin and a thumbs up. Jeremiah giggled as he stood up and began handing out morning assignments to the workforce.

At the Chapel Street apartment in Brooklyn, the girls were sitting tight that morning. They would drive past H.T. headquarters again in the afternoon, before they met with Noah. Sephora didn't want to take a chance riding the subway, at least until the team had more information regarding Degarne. Once Noah and the Intelligence Department in Pittsburgh, had a better handle on his whereabouts, then they would resume their hook up with Repoh or Rue. Serafina and Michaela knew it was the best thing to do, but it made Michaela crazy. Much like Noah, she didn't like to sit still either. It was funny, because she was a lot like Noah, although he made her nuts too. Serafina and Sephora sat quietly and thought about the mission, in hopes that everything went smoothly next time with Repoh. Michaela played with a deck of cards on the coffee table. She had been shuffling and tapping the deck on the table, then she reshuffled and tapped again. Serafina raised an eyebrow at Michaela. It was almost like she had heard it. Michaela set the cards down and sulked like a bored kid. "Are we going to just sit here all day?" she asked, looking toward Sephora.

"Michaela, we need to be careful for now. Yes, we will wait until this afternoon to go out. Hopefully, Noah will be able to tell us something more."

"There's nothing to do," Michaela said, frowning.

"Why don't you take a walk around the neighborhood?" Sephora replied. "Maybe Serafina will walk with you."

"Excuse me?" Serafina smirked.

"Or not," Sephora said.

"Oh, come on," Serafina said, as she stood, "if it will keep you quiet for a little while."

Michaela smiled and followed Serafina out of the apartment. That pleased Sephora, because she would have some quiet time to contemplate a plan for the evening.

Thomas called Mark later in the morning to collaborate. Mark told Thomas that as far as anyone knew, Degarne was still inside H.T. headquarters in New York City. No one had seen him leave the structure since he was seen entering the night before. Thomas retorted that the west coast office was still keeping tabs on Regna. Thomas expressed some doubt whether Regna was shadowing the Broken employees in Hollywood. Regna had been spending a lot of time in North Hollywood, mainly on Camarillo Street, which was on the other side of town from H.T. headquarters. On all of the sightings of Regna, he seemed to be alone, as if he was on a stakeout. Thomas vowed that he would keep his workers on the case until they found out what Regna was up to. He told Mark that he would check, to see if C.O.A. had anyone in the area that Regna could be watching. Before they hung up, each one assured the other that they would report back with any updates as they unfolded.

The A.R. Director and her assistant had been going over a last minute checklist for the employee meeting that was to take place the following day. All decorations were in place and everyone had been apprised of their duties for the meeting. With everything ready for the next day, the two women were relaxing in the conference room discussing the events that had taken place earlier, in the morning. They couldn't help but chuckle about Jonah's debut as the project leader. Although both agreed that he had cleaned up nicely and had stepped up to the job.

By the early afternoon, Jonah was worn out and had gotten bored with trying to act grown up.

"Isn't this day ever going to end?" Jonah whipped.

"I'm proud of you, partner. What's next on the agenda?" Jeremiah asked, as he tried to keep Jonah focused.

"Let's see, we have a couple of young kids playing with matches near a plant in Elizabeth Township," Jonah blurted out as he tugged on his tie again. Two angels moved quickly and took the assignment from Jonah, then went on their way. Jonah pulled another card from the pile and read it. "Okay, next we have an old woman attempting to climb a tree to retrieve her cat. Oh my, that's not gonna end well," Jonah started chanting like an auctioneer. "Do we have any takers? You two in the front row, oh wait, now to the men in the middle. Going once, going twice, sold to the man in the blue suit and woman with the awesome bouffant hairdo, in the fourth row! Come on down." The room snickered as the team stepped up to claim the task from Jonah. Jonah smiled and took a bow. He was back in his glory. Jeremiah glanced at his watch, it was 1:45 p.m. He thought to himself that things were going better than he could have imagined with Jonah. They were past the halfway point by then. As long as he could keep Jonah focused, they just might make it through the day without any hiccups. There were a few side bets going on within C.O.A. to the contrary, but Jeremiah's money was on his partner!

Gabriel and Sarah met Josh again, at the East Side Baptist Church for the afternoon meeting. The team conveyed to Josh the positive feedback that they had received. The news lifted a weight off of Josh's shoulders. As was the night before, people were waiting inside. There were ten attendees at the time. The team followed behind Josh, into the room. As the team located a seat, they saw Seil, seated in the back. He looked as arrogant as ever. Gabriel tried to keep his cool when Seil nodded and smiled, without a word.

As Josh quietly introduced himself, Seil sized Josh up. He was tall, lanky, and lacked confidence. How much easier could it be, he thought? At first, Josh was rattled by some of the comments that Seil had tried to hurl at Josh regarding religion. Sarah told Gabriel to let Josh handle the situation, so he kept quiet. The more Seil hammered Josh with rebuttals, the more upset he became with the recruiter, but his conviction never wavered. Seil continued to argue with Josh on every issue. A few of the walking souls who had been undecided beforehand seemed to take an interest in Seil and his views. Gabriel became fidgety. Finally, Josh, having had enough of Seil, paused, then calmly said, "Sir, if all you want to do is argue, then I'm going to have to ask you to leave. This is a discussion group, not a trial!"

"No problem, I need a smoke anyway," Seil replied, with unruffled indifference, as he exited the room. He winked at Gabriel on the way out, with two new recruits following behind him. Seil had found that Josh Alexander wasn't such an easy target after all, but took comfort in the fact that he'd reined in two more victims.

Sarah was right all along. Josh handled the situation better than Gabriel could've imagined. Even though Seil, once again, had gotten under Gabriel's skin, he preferred to think of the situation as a success for Josh.

Back in New York, Michaela had made it through her boring day. The girls took a few passes by the H.T. building, before they headed to Starbucks for the 5 p.m. meeting, with Noah. There were still no surprises at H.T. headquarters. As was the case the day before, a guard was still posted outside the building. He was still annoying the animals in the green slime. Although at that time, the sentry had been tossing stones to them and laughing as they found out it wasn't food. The monsters were not amused as they snorted and growled at the guard. Michaela couldn't help but wish that the guard had gotten just a little too close to the edge as they drove around the block.

Noah and the girls arrived at the coffee shop at the same time. Everyone bought a coffee, then picked a table in the back, as usual. As they sat down Michaela spoke first, "Please tell us that we are not still on hold, Noah."

"I'm afraid so," Noah replied nervously. "We know that Degarne spent most of the day in the office, but we were informed not long ago that he was out and about again. We are not sure what he's up to, but we expect that he will be riding the subway again."

Michaela groaned and dropped her head to the table, which made Noah start tapping his coffee cup anxiously on the table.

"We understand Noah," Sephora spoke up. "Better safe than sorry."

Serafina nodded in agreement. Michaela lifted her head up with a curled up lip, but didn't protest.

"I promise, as soon as I hear that it's safe, we are back to business." Noah said, trying to sound cheerful, as Michaela rolled her eyes. Noah stood up to leave, looked at his watch and said, "Okay then, tomorrow, 5 p.m. we will meet at Dunkin Donuts on Myrtle Avenue. It's close to your apartment and runs parallel to Flushing."

"Sounds good Noah. We'll find it," Sephora replied, as the team got up to leave too.

CHAPTER 18

The next morning was busy at C.O.A. Pittsburgh. After the early morning assignments were taken care of, everyone would head to the ninety-ninth floor, to the all employee meeting. Employees from the satellite offices in the area would fill in for C.O.A. employees' duties, so that they could attend the meeting. The project leaders of the day were coordinating with the fill ins to make sure all jobs would be covered for the day. Once they were satisfied that everything was under control, the workforce headed upstairs.

The A.R. Director and her assistant greeted the workers as they funneled into the auditorium. There was a long banner above the entrance that read, Project Lost Faith. The whole inside of the auditorium had been spotlessly cleaned. The flooring was light tan colored ceramic tile, with dark brown swirls entwined throughout. All of the wood throughout the auditorium was hand carved mahogany, which included the baseboards, crown molding, and pews. There were little wooden doors at the end of each pew with precisely detailed, hand carved designs as well. The ceiling was approximately thirty feet high in the auditorium, decorated with a beautiful, vibrant collage of scenes from the bible. The paintings were so meticulous that they looked lifelike.

A choir of one hundred angels was seated in the choir loft, patiently waiting for the festivities to begin. The choir, along with the organist, were dressed in white robes and a lavender sash wrapped over their shoulders. The organist quietly played hymns at a low volume, while everyone siphoned into the room and found a seat. The organ itself was made of stunning polished mahogany with six-hundred-ten pipes. It was almost twenty feet high, and spanned from the choir loft floor to the ceiling of the auditorium.

Sunlight beamed through the colorful stained-glass windows and the diamond chandelier sparkled as well, lighting up the room. To the right side of the altar, a podium was set up where selected employees would speak to the workforce. Once everyone was in place, the A.R. Director would start the meeting and announce the speakers. The auditorium was almost three-quarters full and the employees were talking amongst themselves. The organist noticed that the chatter had been getting louder as the room filled up, so he turned up the volume, just a little on the organ.

Jonah, Jeremiah and Jonah's shadow, Theo, took a seat next to Gabriel and Sarah. Jeremiah introduced the newbie to Gabriel and Sarah. They exchanged pleasantries and small talk as they waited for the A. R. Director to begin the meeting. Jonah mentioned to Sarah that Gabriel seemed to have something on his mind. Sarah told Jonah about the run in with Seil, but she assured Jonah it would be fine. Jonah knew that Seil had been a thorn in Gabriel's side for a long time. Jonah had no use for Seil either, but it really bothered him when his friends were effected by Seil's behavior.

Theo was excited to be attending his first all employee meeting. Being new, he soaked everything in as it happened. Especially when Jonah had his ear. Jonah had taken Theo under his wing like a mother bird. Jonah had told Theo to calm down and not to be so fidgety, so Theo folded his hands on his lap and tried to relax. Jeremiah got a kick out of watching the two of them.

At a few minutes before 10 a.m. the director poked her head out to see if everyone was in place and had taken their seats. At that point, the room was almost 90% full. A few minutes later she reappeared for a second look. There were a few people still trickling in, but the room was just about full. The director nodded to the organist, who in turn gave a queue to the choir. They stood in unison and immediately began singing the hymn "How Great Thou Art" in perfect harmony. With that, the workforce instantly became silent and turned their attention toward the choir loft. The acoustics in the auditorium were great. The organ boomed in perfect synchronization with the choir. Everyone was mesmerized by the breathtaking performance.

During the presentation, a wonderful light entered the room and began to dance in the air above the employees. The entire room let out a gasp of joy. The colorful light enveloped the whole auditorium. The colors were amazing and included every shade imaginable. It was like the Northern Lights, but way more astonishing, if you could perceive that. God's spirit had entered the room at that point, and everyone was captivated. All of the angels felt His presence and were filled with joy. Theo was so overwhelmed, that he was about to bust. Jonah patted Theo's shoulder and smiled like a proud father. The angels knew that God was everywhere, but it was always special to them when His presence was exhibited during these conferences. He would be present for the entire meeting, but would not take control. He would let the employees take the reins, but was always available for guidance.

At the end of the song, the A.R. Director stepped up to the podium, tapped the microphone and spoke up. "How about a hand for the choir?" The audience applauded and a few people whistled. As the crowd quieted, she said, "And especially for our C.E.O.!" Then she raised her arms in acknowledgement. The entire room stood and cheered as the magnificent lights danced again throughout the auditorium. Once everyone had settled down, the director took to the podium again and started the meeting. She reminded the group that the reason they were there that day was for a cause close to the C.E.O.'s heart, Project Lost Faith. She then introduced the first speaker, Marketing Department Supervisor Benjamin.

Benjamin outlined several undertakings that had taken place within his department, to enhance interest among the walking souls and win them over. He mentioned the headway that Gabriel and Sarah had made, along with the many other employees, which generated applause. He went on to explain how it had become "not cool" for many young people to believe in God. That was extremely painful, not only to the C.E.O., but the whole corporation as well. Benjamin ended his speech like a football coach with, "With God on our side, we can overturn this growing trend. We won't rest until the Broken have been defeated!" The crowd stood and applauded once more, as Benjamin left the podium. The A.R. Director announced to everyone that they were free to make suggestions, after all of the speakers had finished their speeches, then she announced the next speaker.

All of the departments at C.O.A., had been represented during the assembly. Each one of the supervisors talked about how their units could help the cause, then offered their recommendations on how to combat the task at hand. Everyone had very positive ideas to share. Teamwork was one of C.O.A.'s greatest assets, and also what everyone loved about their company. There was no competition or rivalry between the employees, which made it an enjoyable atmosphere for one and all.

After all of the department heads finished speaking, the floor was open for questions and comments. It had been like an enormous brainstorming session. Many good ideas were offered up. The main focus was on how to infiltrate social media sites that many young people communicated through in those days. One item that seemed to go over well with the employees was creating a nonviolent video game for kids. One that revolves around being rewarded for certain selfless deeds, which would move the player to the next level of the game. The I.T. Department seemed to be pleased with the idea. They promised to put a team of programmers on the project straightaway.

Another idea that had been batted around was to come up with a catchy slogan for social media. They wanted something with a hook. Most people agreed that "Pay It Forward" had been one of the better phrases that had popped up in the recent past that everyone had heard of. It had a lot of momentum for a while with many people jumping on the bandwagon. During chatter back and forth, one of the employees shouted out, "With indifference everywhere, dare to be different. Believe." Everyone thought it was great. It was catchy and easy to remember. If it worked, it would turn the tables and make it cool to go your own route, instead of following along with the crowd. The catchphrase was accepted by a sign of applause. The Art Department would get to work on a design for billboards and the websites directly after the meeting.

Content with the results of the conference, the A.R. Director thanked everyone for attending and closed the meeting with a nod to the organist. The choir stood once again and sang "What a friend we have in Jesus" as the crowd dispersed from the auditorium and returned to their work stations. The attendees seemed to be pumped up with the new promotions, and couldn't wait to see the results. They were still exchanging ideas between themselves as they exited the room. Each of the employees would have a small wrap up meeting with project leaders within their department to review assignments related to the mission.

Later that afternoon, Noah met with the girls at the Dunkin Donuts in Flushing, promptly at five o'clock. It was not good news. The encounter was short, but not so sweet. The team would need to sit tight again in New York. Noah explained that they didn't have a lock on Degarne yet, but felt confident that he would have better news the next morning. They would meet at the same place at 9 a.m. Noah scurried out of the coffee shop before Michaela could stare him down.

CHAPTER 19

Early the next morning, Mark and his people had found footage of Degarne leaving New York City, headed east toward Pennsylvania, alone. The Intelligence Department would keep tabs on him as closely as they could. Mark called Thomas to find out if there had been any news on the west coast, regarding Regna. Thomas said that they were still tracking Regna. He was still travelling back and forth, between North Hollywood and H.T. headquarters. Thomas still hadn't been able to pinpoint what Regna's curiosity was in North Hollywood, but assured Mark he was having Regna shadowed closely. Before they hung up, Mark told Thomas that Degarne was on the move, and he would contact Thomas later in the morning.

With the departure of Degarne from H.T. headquarters in New York, tension among the H.T. employees had seemed to ease up just a tad. At least the closed door meetings between the leaders had subsided for the time being. Although Soahc and Covah had shown more of a presence as they popped in and out of different departments throughout the morning. Probably just to keep the workers on their toes. Even with Degarne gone from the building, chatter was at a minimum with Soahc and Covah on the prowl.

When Noah entered the Donut shop on Myrtle Avenue, the girls had already arrived and were sitting at a table. Before he had a chance to open his mouth, Michaela blurted out, "Tell us that you have good news, Noah."

"As a matter of fact, I do," Noah replied with a smile.

Sephora and Serafina let out a sigh of relief in unison, which prompted a raised eyebrow from Michaela.

"We received information this morning, that Degarne is heading east, through Pennsylvania right now. Possibly making his way to Pittsburgh. We feel confident that you are safe to return to the subway, at least for tonight," Noah announced happily.

"Phew, you don't know how happy that makes us, Noah. I couldn't take another night with this one moping around," Serafina said, with a tilted head toward Michaela.

"Hey!" Michaela spouted out.

Before Michaela had time to respond further, Sephora spoke up, "That's great news Noah. Hopefully we can reach out to Repoh tonight. Where and when do we meet next?"

Noah glanced at his watch and replied, "Nine, tomorrow morning, unless something comes up. Let's meet at Joe's Diner on 2nd Avenue, in East Village."

With all in agreement, Michaela jumped to her feet before Noah had finished his sentence. Given Michaela's restlessness, he waved the girls on ahead. He would wait for a few minutes until they had gone before exiting the coffee shop. Serafina rolled her eyes without Michaela seeing the gesture, then Sephora smiled at Noah on the way out.

Gabriel and Sarah spent the morning at the gym, working out with their friends in the North Hills. They discussed the next meeting with Josh Alexander. They asked the walking souls to contemplate an interesting idea to bring new people to the meeting. They all agreed to put their heads together to work on something. Gabriel and Sarah already had plans to meet with Josh after their morning workout. The team would brainstorm with Josh and give the illusion that Josh had helped come up with the slogan that had already been decided upon during the C.O.A. meeting. Gabriel and Sarah had no doubt that Josh would run with the idea and add it to his flyers. It would boost Josh's confidence level and help to enhance his leadership qualities among the attendees as well.

Jeremiah, Jonah and Theo were finishing up an assignment in Bloomfield. A small neighborhood bar was badly in need of repairs, but the owner didn't have the money to update the electrical system. The bar wasn't scheduled to open for a few more hours, when some loose wiring started sparking in the kitchen. An apartment building was adjoined to the bar, which housed ten families. If the angels had waited for the firemen to arrive it would've been too late, and everyone in the building would have been homeless…or worse. Of course, Theo hung on every word as Jonah explained the repairs to him. The team had made the bar safe again, at least for the time being. Before leaving the business, Jeremiah sat one-thousand dollars on the bar with an anonymous note to the owner to call an electrician. Then they slipped out the back door unnoticed.

Mark and his team had eyes on Degarne, who had made his way to Pittsburgh as the intelligence team had presumed he would. He didn't spend time in any one place, but had been spotted in several locations along the rivers, in the city. They would continue to monitor his whereabouts so they could report back to New York, regarding his departure from Pittsburgh. Thomas and his team were still watching Regna, who continued to travel back and forth between Hollywood and North Hollywood. He still seemed most interested in Camarillo Street. Thomas' team were narrowing down businesses in the area to find out what could be of such an importance to Regna.

Gabriel and Sarah had met with Josh Alexander. The team told Josh how proud they were of him, the way he took charge and handled Seil at the last meeting. Josh blushed a little and thanked the team for their support. Josh took to the slogan idea right away, and was excited to implement it onto the new flyers. Everything worked as the team had planned. The three of them had created a template on Josh's computer. Gabriel copied the document onto a flash drive and told Josh that he would get copies of flyers made, then return them to Josh later in the day, to be distributed. He would also give several copies to their clients from the gym and leave some at the front desk of the fitness center.

The girls made a pass by H.T.'s building in New York before they headed out for a long night, riding the subway. The same H.T. guard was on patrol of the building, and the moat was down again, but another sentry had been posted with him at that time. As was the case on the last trip, they were torturing the monsters in the green slime liquid. One of the employees had an old stick with a shoe hanging from it and he was dangling the shoe over the animals. He yanked it back just as the beasts snapped at what they thought was their dinner. It kept the guards amused and they didn't seem to care about anything else at that moment. Confident that things looked as normal as possible with H.T., the girls turned the car towards the subway stop at Penn Station.

Sephora, Serafina and Michaela rode the train for approximately eight hours without any sighting of Repoh. Even though the night had been a bust so far, Serafina was comforted by the fact that she didn't have to spend another evening sitting in the apartment with Michaela whining. It had been decided that Serafina would be the one to make contact with Repoh on that evening. Although Degarne was out of New York, the team didn't want anyone else to see Repoh and Sephora recognized together, after the last incident. The three would board one train, then depart and climb aboard another subway car a few stops later. Each of the girls separated into adjoining cars. They would repeat the process until they finally ran into Repoh at close to midnight near Times Square.

Serafina, nonchalantly took a seat behind Repoh. He had recognized Serafina before she sat down. She scanned the other passengers in the car for beady red eyes. There were no other Broken, besides Repoh aboard. She waited a few minutes as she double checked the passengers. Everyone was either half asleep or too wrapped up in their own problems to pay attention to either Serafina or Repoh.

Serafina opted not to waste time on small talk. "Degarne is in Pittsburgh."

"I heard he was out of the area," Repoh replied. "Wasn't sure where, though."

"C.O.A. has eyes on him. He's spending a lot of time near the rivers. Any idea why?" Serafina asked.

"He's had a lot of closed meetings with upper management lately. Word is that he's concocting something huge, but not much has leaked out, other than Pittsburgh, being involved." Repoh continued, "I am keeping my ears open. Let me see what I can find out and we can hook up again tomorrow night. I will make it a point to be near Penn Station around midnight tomorrow."

"Have you spoken to Rue?" Serafina inquired.

"Not lately. Too risky for now," Repoh answered.

"We would like to touch base with him also," Serafina replied, then waited for Repoh's thoughts.

"Be careful. He spooks easily, especially knowing that Degarne has been lurking around. You should be able to find him near Central Park." Repoh replied hesitantly.

"We were told that he would most likely be near the park. We were thinking maybe tomorrow, as long as Degarne remains out of the picture," Serafina responded as she stood to make the next stop, "Until tomorrow night, then," she whispered as she passed Repoh. The three girls exited the separate cars in unison, while Repoh gazed out the window on the opposite side of the exit.

CHAPTER 20

The west coast employee meeting had gone just as well as the Pittsburgh conference in the east. Not only had San Francisco embraced the east coast slogan, *With indifference everywhere, dare to be different. Believe,* but expanded upon it with, *Don't follow others blindly. Be the messenger. Believe.* Both coasts had already inundated the social media sites with the new slogans. Print shops worked nonstop and billboards had already been raised on the east coast in populated metropolitan cities, and the west coast would be following suit the next day. The goal was to hit it hard and fast before the Broken had a chance to notice. C.O.A. knew that it wouldn't be long after, that H.T. would try to find a way to combat the offensive.

Gabriel and Sarah had returned to Josh Alexander's residence with a stack of flyers for him to hand out. Sarah told Josh about the billboards, so that he wouldn't be caught off guard. Josh couldn't believe that the team had been able to put together such a huge undertaking in so little time. The team assured Josh that they had friends in high places who worked fast. Sarah expressed to Josh that they would like to use him as a contact for anyone interested in starting a similar group in other cities. Josh graciously accepted the offer and promised to help in any way he could.

The intelligence team in San Francisco was still tracking Regna. They had been researching some of the businesses near Camarillo Street, since Regna seemed so interested in that area. There were a lot of studios in the vicinity along with a few theatres. It was an urban, artsy type area. An old dance theatre was currently being renovated on Camarillo Street. The building was about fifty years old and was getting a facelift. It had been empty for the last five years. Construction workers had been observed coming and going all week. They seemed to be in a hurry to finish the renovations. C.O.A. had pinpointed that block as a frequent hangout for Regna. Although the team couldn't figure out why Regna would be so concerned with an old theatre.

Mark and his team still had eyes on Degarne, who, unlike Regna, didn't spend much time in any one place. He had moved all around Point State Park, or just the Point, as Pittsburghers refer to it. It was where the Allegheny, Monongahela and Ohio rivers came together. In the near vicinity were Heinz Field, PNC Park, and a riverboat fleet, along with many businesses, not to mention the bridges in the area. Degarne could be scouting any of those locations. No one could be sure, since he was continually moving around. C.O.A. employees were asked to steer clear of the Point while Degarne was in town. The team didn't want anything to chase him out of the city before they could find out what he was up to.

Sephora, Serafina and Michaela had met with Noah at the diner that morning, as previously planned. Serafina gave her report to Noah regarding the meeting with Repoh. Noah was glad the team had finally been able to make contact. Sephora expressed to Noah their eagerness to meet with Rue as soon as possible. Noah was in agreement with them, but advised the girls to be cautious. As Repoh had brought up, Rue was not as composed when stressed. The girls promised to be watchful. Before they left the diner, Sephora told Noah about the upcoming meeting with Repoh later in the evening as well. Hopefully, he would have more information as well. Noah scheduled a meeting for the next morning with the girls before he left the diner.

With Degarne and Regna on the prowl, C.O.A. soldiers were again on hand at each of the headquarters. With the conclusion of the employee meetings, the conference rooms were not being used. The soldiers had been occupying the rooms for the time being. The generals were told to have the troops at the ready, but to keep a low profile. The conference room was the perfect place for the soldiers to stay out of the way. The only other employees accessing the rooms would be the A.R. Directors and a small cleanup crew. Most of the workforce wouldn't even notice them, except when Generals James or Luke went between the conference room and the Intelligence Department, for updates on the H.T. moles.

Jonah didn't notice the army presence in the building at that time, which suited them just fine. The sergeants were not posted in the lobby as they had been previously. Besides, Jonah was much too busy mentoring Theo to worry about anything else. With Jonah paying so much attention to Theo, Jeremiah didn't have to exert so much energy keeping Jonah out of trouble. It was something that Jeremiah longed for at times, but at that moment he sort of missed the chaos. He had grown so used to watching over Jonah for so long that it had become second nature. Jeremiah's phone rang while Jonah was mentoring Theo. When he hung up, he announced that the project leader had an assignment for the team.

It turned out, that an up and coming young politician was having a stent put in. Jerome Rodgers was a Councilman in District 6, which covered the lower Hill District in Pittsburgh. He was recovering from a recent heart attack. Jeremiah had been selected to oversee the operation scheduled by a prominent surgeon in the city. Under normal circumstances, the operation would have been second nature to the specialist. That week had been exceptionally busy for the doctor. He was functioning on very little sleep, between a heavy workload and a few distractions in his personal life. Jeremiah was to make sure no mistakes were made during the procedure.

Councilman Rodgers was a happily married man with two young children. He had proved to be an advocate for family values, educational reform and retraining displaced workers in the city. He was a well-respected figure in his district. His popularity had also prompted the attention of some prominent state leaders. He was on a path to move up the political ladder. C.O.A. didn't want a tired surgeon to hinder the progress that the esteemed civil servant had made in the city.

Jonah and Theo waited outside the operating room while Jeremiah stood behind the doctor and remained invisible to the team of doctors. Every once in a while Jeremiah would whisper in the ear of the lead surgeon. Mainly he would remind the doctor to double check each procedure as he went along. During the operation the councilman had been sedated, but was in a twilight type of sleep. He looked a little puzzled during the operation, and the doctor asked if everything was okay. Jerome nodded his head yes, but didn't speak at that time. The surgeon finished the operation successfully, then one of his team wheeled the patient into a recovery room next door. At that point, Jeremiah, Jonah and Theo left the hospital and made their way back to C.O.A. headquarters. Theo had been totally impressed with Jeremiah's performance. Of course, Jonah jokingly exclaimed that he had taught Jeremiah everything he knew.

A few hours later the doctor came to check on Jerome.

"How are you feeling?" The surgeon inquired.

"I'm sore, and a little confused." Jerome replied.

"The soreness, I can understand, but what's confusing to you?" The doctor asked.

"Who was the guy in the suit?" Jerome asked, befuddled.

"Excuse me?" The surgeon enquired, seemingly bewildered.

"I saw a man in a suit behind you, whispering in your ear during the procedure," Jerome continued. "I could see him clear as day!"

"No, there was no one but my team in the room, and they wore surgical gowns. Maybe it was your guardian angel," the doctor responded.

"Or yours!" Jerome shot back.

"Could be. You never know. Come back and see me for a checkup in two weeks." The doctor smiled and patted Jerome on the leg as he left the room. As the doctor left, he remembered that he'd seen Jerome look past him with a bewildered gaze. He paused, reached into his pocket and pulled out one of Josh Alexander's flyers, which displayed the new slogan at the top. The doctor wondered how the flyer ended up in his pocket, then muttered to himself, "Hmm, you never know." The surgeon then returned the flyer to his pocket. With nothing scheduled for the next twenty-four hours, the doctor decided he would go home and get a good night's sleep for a change.

At dusk, Serafina drove Sephora and Michaela past H.T. in New York, to make sure nothing had changed. At the time, two guards who looked bored were sitting on opposite sides of the door. Apparently they had grown tired of torturing the creatures under the moat. Another possibility could have been that the animals had wised up and realized that the sentries were just tormenting them. With all things normal, the team then made their way to Central Park.

The girls split up as much as they could, but stayed within eyesight of each other. A few hours had passed when they noticed Rue, as he sat alone on a park bench, feeding bread crumbs to some attentive pigeons. The team scanned the area for ten minutes, just to make sure there were no other prying red eyes in the area. Sephora mentioned that Rue's eyes were lighter, almost pinkish. She had noticed the same with Repoh. It was a little odd, because most of the Broken had a bright red glow in their eyes.

Once the team was satisfied, Michaela approached Rue from his side, out of his peripheral vision. "Rue?" She asked quietly.

Michaela had startled Rue, and he threw the breadcrumbs into the air, which in turn also frightened the birds. Once they saw all of the bread hit the ground, the birds recovered and scrambled for their share.

"Sorry. I'm Michaela."

"I thought you were taller," Rue spouted as he brushed the crumbs from his pants. He looked just like the picture that was shown to the girls, shoulder length unkempt hair and a two day beard. He wore a tee shirt and cargo pants.

"Well, I'm not the one who jumped like a little girl!" Michaela shot back.

"Okay, truce?" Rue replied with an apologetic grin.

"Fine. So what's new, anything?" Michaela asked.

"Yes. I've heard some shop talk that H.T. has been working with a few walking souls. One is a businessman from New York. The other is a preacher. I'm not sure where he is from."

"A preacher?" Michaela replied with a puzzled look.

"That's what I hear," Rue said, shrugging his shoulders.

Michaela turned her gaze toward her partners, to make sure the coast was clear. Both girls nodded to Michaela, giving her the okay.

"Any idea what these walking souls are being used for?" Michaela inquired.

"Not yet, but I'll listen for any juicy gossip around the water cooler, so to speak."

"Thanks Rue." Michaela continued, "We are meeting Repoh in an hour or so."

Rue's ears perked up. "Tell him I said hello."

"We will," Michaela agreed. "Got to go for now. Next time I'll try not to sneak up on you!"

Rue laughed, "I'd appreciate that. Talk to you later."

The girls made their way back to the Cavalier, where they had left it, at the edge of the park. They drove to a subway stop at Cathedral Parkway, then took the train south, toward Penn Station to meet Repoh. A little after midnight, the girls had spotted Repoh near Canal Street. Sephora took a seat behind Repoh. He was the only one in the train car for the moment. She told him that Rue said hello. Repoh was happy to hear that he was okay. She informed him of the newfound information regarding the walking souls.

"The businessman makes sense. I've heard chatter that a walking soul was involved with Degarne somehow. It probably has to do with his visit to Pittsburgh. Although, the preacher is news to me. I'm not sure where he fits in, but I'll see what I can find out," Repoh said, as he kept his eyes straight forward.

"We will give our intelligence team the newest information. You both have been a great help. Between you, Rue, and our team, we will get to the root of it. We will keep in touch." Repoh nodded without a response. Sephora stood as the train came to another stop. Two passengers were boarding as she passed by them in the doorway, then disappeared.

The trio felt like they had finally made some progress. They would call Mark in Pittsburgh, when they returned to the apartment, to let him know that they had news, but Noah could handle the sensitive data on a secure phone line in the morning. Hopefully the intelligence team would get the name of the businessman, and the mysterious preacher that seemed to have everyone baffled at the moment.

CHAPTER 21

The eight o'clock meetings the next morning were busy as usual, but there was a lot of buzz about Project Lost Faith. Many of the employees were talking about billboards popping up all over the area. The I.T. Department had noticed a lot of circulation on multiple social media sites as well. Gabriel and Sarah had met with their supervisor and notified him of how busy Josh Alexander had been in the past few days. The team would be trying to recruit help for Josh from their friends at the gym, as well as former clients. Benjamin expressed delight with the growth in participation, and had agreed with the team's assessment. They had his full support.

The girls met with Noah that morning and passed on the information that had been attained from Repoh and Rue. Noah promised to relay the findings to Mark in Pittsburgh, as soon as he'd returned to the office. Noah revealed that he hadn't received any reports of Repoh leaving the city at that point, so the girls should be fine to contact Repoh and Rue. Another meet with Noah was set up for the following morning, then the girls returned to the apartment. They planned to return to the park, to find Rue after dark.

Mark and the intelligence team were trying to find out what they could about the mystery men from the new information. An afternoon phone call from Thomas in San Francisco helped out somewhat. Thomas and his team had looked into the old dance theatre that had been getting a facelift on Camarillo Street. What interested the team was how fast the construction was being completed, and with a huge team of workers. The new owner was Jedidiah Compton Ministries. Jedidiah was an evangelistic minister with a growing following. Regna hadn't been seen with Jedidiah, but the team seemed confident that he was Regna's contact. At that point, the team waited for more concrete evidence before deciding how to proceed. For safety reasons, the army presence had been increased at C.O.A. San Francisco.

Jedidiah Compton was a tall, good looking, people person. He easily gained people's confidence with his charms. As a young man, he spent some time in jail for petty larceny. He had found it easy to cheat people with bogus schemes. He was the kind of person that you wanted to trust, and he took advantage of that fact. Even in his ministry, he was able to convince his followers that he was a changed man. C.O.A. was not so easily fooled by a pretty face. If he was up to something, they would uncover it.

Jerimiah and Jonah took advantage of a lull in the action, and took Theo to the warehouse in the Strip District. Of course Jonah took a detour, to show the newbie Primanti Brothers restaurant on the way. The team had given Theo the tour of all of Jonah's favorite toys in the warehouse. Theo was shown the requisition and return authorization forms needed, when acquiring vehicles from the clerk. Before leaving, of course Jonah had to climb into one of the race cars. Jeremiah and the supply clerk waited patiently to watch Jonah peel himself from the car. As Jonah's legs dangled, Theo yanked at his feet, trying to help. As usual, Jonah wound up with his shirt wrapped around his head.

"Never gets old, huh?" The clerk asked, grinning.

"Like watching a skunk with a can stuck on his head!" Jeremiah replied, arms crossed.

Since the team didn't need to rush back to the office, Jonah proposed a stop by the Sunny Days Nursing home to pay another visit to Rose Light. Jeremiah agreed that it would be a nice surprise for Rose. Jonah thought it would be good for Theo to have a chance to interact with the walking souls. When the team entered the nursing home they were greeted with warm welcomes. Well, at least Jonah was. The old folks shouted his name and Jonah ate it up as he strutted in like a movie star! Rose's eyes lit up as she stood to greet him with a hug.

The team hadn't noticed Seil when they entered the room.

"Well, if it isn't Easy Wider and Jeremiah Bond! Who's the newbie?" Seil proclaimed.

Jonah moved toward Seil.

"Easy, Jonah," Jeremiah warned.

Jonah put one arm around Seil's shoulder and moved him around the corner. Before Seil could speak, Jonah pinched Seil's lips between his fingers, "Don't worry about who the newbie is, Seil!"

Seil tried to mumble something, but still had his lips sealed by Jonah.

Jonah continued, "I don't like you messing with my people and I don't like your smug, pretty face. Your mouth really gets you into trouble." Jonah extended a razor sharp nail from his index finger. He placed it on Seil's upper lip. He cut a slit in Seil's lip, about a quarter inch long. Seil grimaced in pain. Jonah finally let go of Seil. The recruiter pulled a handkerchief from his back pocket and held it to his lip.

"Are you crazy?" Seil asked, visibly upset.

"You better get that looked at. It's definitely going to leave a scar!" Jonah exclaimed.

As Seil headed for the exit, Jonah hollered, "See you next time buddy!"

Jeremiah noticed Seil leave with his handkerchief against his mouth, and asked, "What happened, Jonah?"

"Nothing, it's all good," Jonah replied, casually.

Gabriel and Sarah had spent most of the afternoon contacting everyone that they could to help Josh Alexander. Josh was a bit overwhelmed with phone calls from people looking for information regarding his meetings. Sarah had tried to keep Josh focused on the big picture and not to get too anxious. The team had managed to find a few volunteers to handle the phones and e-mails for Josh. Gabriel worked on drumming up interest for another chairperson to take on an overflow meeting. One of the team's gym buddies offered to help with that task. The pastor of East Side Baptist Church was more than happy to share the church for an additional discussion group. Josh seemed to be able to relax some, after seeing how the team had facilitated volunteers.

Project Lost Faith hadn't gone unnoticed by H.T. Enterprises. The Downtrodden, had alerted their foremen all morning about the billboards that had popped up like wild fire. It hadn't taken long before the information had risen through the ranks. Covah summoned Soahc, along with a few high ranking employees for an impromptu gathering with the C.E.O. Mehyam, and designated employees on the west coast would be on the phone for the conversation. Security had not been increased yet, but all employees expected the order to be handed down shortly. For the time being, the outside of H.T. headquarters remained seemingly lax as it had been for the past week or so.

The west coast team first realized that Regna had returned to the Hollywood H.T. office sometime in the afternoon, but had not resurfaced from the building by early evening. He had been bouncing like a yo-yo for the past few days between Camarillo Street and headquarters. Thomas informed Mark of the situation, so that they could keep an eye on Degarne in Pittsburgh. At the time Thomas contacted Mark, the intelligence team was having trouble locating Degarne, which was a strange coincidence. He had last been seen near the river, about an hour earlier. Mark glanced at his watch. It was eight-thirty. Mark thought he had better call Noah, so he could warn the girls in New York.

When Noah received the news from Mark, he became panicked. He called Sephora repeatedly, but the calls went directly to voicemail. Noah's anxiety kicked in along with all of his nervous ticks. Unbeknownst to Noah, Sephora had left the phone on the front seat of the car before the team proceeded into Central Park, hoping to find Rue again. Between messages to Sephora, Noah called Pittsburgh to alert Mark. Noah had hoped Mark would strike down his concerns, but the situation worried Mark also. After all, it was his team. Noah assured Mark that he would touch base when he reached Sephora. Mark informed General James right away. Additional troops were assembled at C.O.A. as backup. The troops that had already been on standby, were ready to roll. General James made a decision not to wait for a call. Two platoons were dispatched to New York. Upon their arrival, Sergeants Mathew and Peter, were to wait outside New York City with their platoons, for further orders.

After roaming Central Park for about an hour, Serafina had spotted Rue. He was seated on a bench, but this time he was not surrounded by pigeons. He was leaning back, apparently admiring the stars on a beautiful clear evening. The park was surprisingly quiet for such a pleasant night. A small breeze blew the leaves of the surrounding trees, which made a light swooshing sound. After surveying the vicinity for a few minutes, Michaela approached Rue. At that time, she entered into his front view, so she didn't catch him off guard. Sephora and Serafina were within a hundred feet on both sides of Michaela and Repoh.

Before Michaela had a chance to say hello, two figures swooped down and snatched them both into the air, then disappeared. Serafina started to take off after them, but Sephora stopped her. Sephora recognized one of the figures as Degarne. Serafina and Sephora both agreed that the other culprit was Soahc. Serafina was ready to fight, but Sephora, not knowing who else could be in the area, opted to notify C.O.A. and let them decide on a plan of action. Sephora suspected that Michaela and Rue would be taken to H.T. headquarters. Serafina and Sephora moved quickly back to the car, to retrieve the phone. Sephora regretted her decision to leave the phone behind, but she would deal with it later. As Serafina started to drive toward the apartment, Sephora told her to change her course and get to the subway station. She wanted to pull Repoh out of circulation if it wasn't already too late. Sephora grabbed the phone and saw the missed calls from Noah, but chose to call Mark first, before making contact with Noah.

Mark told Sephora that troops were in place in New York. He wasn't crazy about the idea of going after Repoh, given the circumstances. Sephora remained adamant about extracting Repoh. Mark finally agreed, but would have soldiers meet her and Serafina on the train. They refused to lose another agent at that point. Sephora agreed that Mark had a good point. She and Serafina would wait for backup, before they approached Repoh.

The girls and their entourage caught up with Repoh near Rockefeller Center. He knew right away that something had gone wrong.

"What happened?" he asked eagerly.

"We will explain on the way, but we need to get you out of here now!" Sephora shouted.

"Tell me now," Repoh demanded.

"Rue and Michaela have been abducted. Let's go!" Sephora nodded to the soldiers and they each took an arm as they pulled him from the train.

"We're going to our safe house in Brooklyn for now," Sephora told him as they sped away. Repoh followed the team, but remained speechless. He was terrified, given these new set of circumstances. Sephora called Noah on the way to Brooklyn. He would meet them at the apartment to regroup.

CHAPTER 22

It was two a.m. and H.T. headquarters in New York, had been sealed up like a tomb. The entrance door was sealed, and several sentries were standing guard outside. For the last few hours, Michaela and Rue had been hidden away in the dungeon with Lucifer's undesirables. Michaela was surprised that they had not been interrogated yet. Either the Broken were trying to make them sweat, or they were still deciding how to proceed. As far as Michaela knew, she was the first angel to be taken there. Rue was not handling the situation well. He had barely spoken a word since the abduction. Michaela was shaken, but not like Rue. She knew her team would get her out. Rue was not sure what his fate would be. The two were in adjoining cells. Michaela comforted Rue the best she could, to keep him calm. She didn't want to say too much, not knowing who was listening. Michaela was short, so her cell wasn't as uncomfortable as it was for Rue. Michaela wasn't sure if claustrophobia was setting in on Rue, or just the whole situation for him.

Sephora, Serafina, Repoh, Noah, Sergeants Peter and Mathew were still at the apartment on Chapel Street. The C.O.A. employees sat at the kitchen table and brainstormed the situation. Soldiers were posted outside. Noah had been in communication with headquarters since the abduction occurred. The command center on the ninety-eighth floor was hectic. Mark and his team had a makeshift blueprint of the H.T. building, and they were discussing the next move with General James and other advisors.

With all of the commotion, Sephora took notice of Repoh. He had been quietly sitting in the living room, in a stupor for a while. "Repoh, are you okay?" Sephora asked.

"Rue is my little brother," Repoh blurted out. Then the room went quiet. "What?" Sephora replied in disbelief. Noah began jingling his keys. Serafina shot him a look, then he instantly quieted down. Sephora immediately recalled the pinkish colored eyes that the two had in common, which made more sense to her now.

"It's not something I bring up. We watch out for each other. With our coworkers constantly at each other's throat, it's nice to know that someone has your back," Repoh continued. "And I let him down again."

"What do you mean, again?" Serafina probed.

"Growing up, we had a horrible childhood. Our father barely came around, and our mother became an alcoholic. Rue and I were on our own most of the time. I had a chip on my shoulder a mile long. An aunt had taken us to church once, when we were young, but I didn't want any part of it. At the time, I did whatever I could to make money. Rue looked up to me, being his older brother. One night I stole a car, and Rue was tagging along. The police chased after us. I was driving too fast around a bend, lost control and we slammed into a concrete wall. We both went through the windshield. I was eighteen and Rue was seventeen. Rue wouldn't be where he is if it wasn't for me." Repoh began to sniffle.

"We're going to figure this out, Repoh," Sephora said as she consoled him. "Don't lose it on me now. Try to think of something we can use regarding the layout inside H.T. headquarters."

That caught Repoh's attention. He regained his composure and Sephora could see his wheels starting to spin. "Let me clear my head and think about it for a minute," Repoh replied.

Thomas knew that Mark had his own problems in Pittsburgh, but thought he would touch base with him anyway. Thomas' team in San Francisco had found out that Jedidiah Compton was planning a grand opening revival in three days, at the remodeled theatre in North Hollywood. The construction workers had worked around the clock to finish the job. A Broken informant had relayed Jedidiah's plan, to one of Thomas' team. Jedidiah had gained some popularity in smaller venues so he decided it was time to move to the next level. Mark was grateful for the call from Thomas, but had his own headaches to deal with.

All C.O.A. employees were on call, and most were confined to the building until further notice. Some exceptions were made for customer service and marketing employees, like Gabriel and Sarah. They were to continue their work on the outside, but be close enough to be called in, if need be. The team would carry on their dealings with the clients at the gym and with Josh Alexander. Project Lost Faith would continue as planned, as if nothing had gone wrong.

***

The cries from the other prisoners had started to get to Michaela, and unnerved Rue as well. "Shut up!" Michaela yelled. It only made things worse with the inmates, until the sound of a door slammed in the distance. They heard footsteps from an approaching guard. The guard slowly dragged his nightstick along the bars as he walked. The inmates quieted down as he came closer. Michaela reached through the bars, lifted Rue's face and smiled to calm him. Rue returned a halfhearted grin.

The guard passed by Michaela without a word, then stopped in front of Rue's cell.

The guard grabbed the back of Rue's collar and asked, "Where's your brother?"

Michaela raised an eyebrow, but remained silent.

"I haven't seen him in weeks," Rue replied, as he pulled away from the guard.

"Hmm, we will find him eventually," the guard responded, then turned around and made his way back down the corridor. He resumed tapping his nightstick on the way out. Once the guard slammed the door, Rue explained to Michaela his relationship with Repoh. The inmate's high-pitched screams started up again, but Michaela didn't bother to mute them. She hoped the noise would muffle the conversation between herself and Rue.

Phone conversation continued, between C.O.A. headquarters and the soldiers at the apartment in Brooklyn. More troops were being sent to New York. General James was in favor of storming H.T. headquarters. Noah, Sephora, and Serafina weren't sure that was the best idea. The blueprints were somewhat sketchy, and H.T. would be ready for a fight. As the discussion continued, both sides gave their point of view. Repoh walked to the kitchen and joined the others at the table.

Repoh listened to both sides of the conversation for a short time, before speaking up, "I may have an idea." Repoh paused for a reaction.

"We could use a good idea right now. Spit it out Repoh," General James bellowed over the phone.

"At H.T. headquarters, the air vents are routed in such a way that you can hear the prisoners all over the building. Management has it set up that way, so that everyone can hear their cries and keep employees in line," Repoh explained.

"I'm listening," General James replied.

"There are openings to the outside of the building on the top front and middle rear side of the building. The openings have a thin metal cover, held on by a few screws," Repoh retorted.

"How much room in the ducts?" Sephora asked, wondering if there was enough room for the soldiers.

"It will be tight, but doable," Repoh replied confidently. "Right now, my bosses may be wondering if you have taken me, but don't know for sure. They won't be expecting an assault through the ventilation system. Patrols will have the perimeter surrounded, but the exhaust vents won't be a priority."

"I like it," General James answered. "We will attack the front door with the majority of our forces, while two small teams sneak through the air ducts. The additional troops should arrive to your location shortly. We will go over the details then. I want this finished before daybreak. Good job, Repoh!"

"Thank you General," Repoh replied.

Covah, Soahc, Degarne, Lucifer and a few high ranking soldiers had just adjourned from a closed meeting. Although the consensus was that Repoh had been taken by C.O.A., Degarne was ordered to scout areas that Repoh was known to frequent. H.T. wanted him brought in, if he was still in the vicinity. Covah and Soahc were to make sure their army was ready for an expected retaliation from C.O.A. Covah and Soahc moved quickly, assigning stations for the soldiers, while an alarm sounded throughout the building, to notify employees of high alert status. The C.E.O. returned to his office, then made a call to Mehyam in Hollywood, to apprise him of the situation in New York and advise him to be on guard for any suspicious activity on his end.

In Pittsburgh, a decision had been made in the middle of the night to condense the eight o'clock morning meetings. The project leaders were only to send workers into the field under dire circumstances. The majority of employees were to be restricted to headquarters until further notice.

CHAPTER 23

By four-thirty a.m., C.O.A. employees were prepared for action. Additional troops had made their way to Brooklyn. Repoh was obstinate in his demand to lead the way through the air ducts, on the back end of H.T. He argued that he would get the team in and out more rapidly than they could move on their own, since he was more familiar with the building. General James reluctantly agreed to the plan. With Rue's life depending on it, General James knew that Repoh had a lot riding on the outcome.

Upon arrival at H.T. headquarters, the platoon leaders had relayed their assessment to General James, in Pittsburgh. There were a handful of soldiers on the roof. Troops were also stationed around the building, on the ground. As Repoh had indicated, there were no guards near the air vent openings. Sergeant Mathew would send half of a platoon to attack the soldiers on the roof. He would lead the remaining half on an assault to the back of the building. Sergeant Peter would move in with the other two platoons, then hit the front of the building hard. The militia would strike simultaneously at all three locations.

Repoh and two soldiers would make their way to the air vent in the rear of the building, once the battle had begun. Sephora, Serafina and two other soldiers would enter through the front air vent. Sephora raised an eyebrow to Repoh as if to ask, "are you ready?" Repoh nodded without saying a word. The order was given by General James, then a war cry rang out from the troops.

The soldiers hit the front door hard, which brought the H.T. troops scrambling toward them, as they tried to protect the entry. The rest of the C.O.A. militia hit the roof, and back of the building. With all of the confusion, Repoh and his team headed for the back air vent. The girls and sentries made their way toward the front air vent. Everyone was too busy to notice either of the extraction teams, as they ripped the covers off and entered the vents.

The Broken tried to hold their ground at the front entrance, but they were taking on many injuries. The C.O.A. soldiers were pummeling the Broken army. One of the sentries that had previously been torturing the animals in the pond had been tossed into the green slime. He was torn to pieces before he even hit the water. The guards outside on the roof had been taken care of, and the roof was secured. A group of guards waited patiently inside for the C.O.A. soldiers to break through, at the top of the building. General James told them to hold their position. The general wanted to keep the Broken sentries guessing. They wouldn't need to go inside the roof entrance, if all worked to plan.

Repoh had made good time through the air vents, as the soldiers in tow tried to keep up. It was a tight squeeze for them, since they were much bigger than Repoh. Sephora and Serafina led the assault on the other end. Sephora had memorized the route that Repoh had explained to her and Serafina. The screams of the inmates had gotten louder as the teams made their way closer to the dungeon. No one had followed them, so everything was going as intended.

The C.O.A. soldiers had pushed the Broken, from the back of the building toward the sides and front of the structure. The noise was extremely loud. The angel warriors continued their war cries. The Broken couldn't hear their commanding officer's orders over the uproar, so they became confused. Some of the Broken abandoned their posts. Others did the best they could to hold back the angels at the front door.

As Repoh and the two soldiers reached the dungeon, they stopped and scoped out the area, before they climbed out of the duct. Repoh didn't see any sign of guards, which he found somewhat peculiar. He stepped out as quietly as possible, then the soldiers followed behind him. Across the way, Repoh noticed Sephora and her team emerging from the vent as well.

"Rue?" Repoh whispered.

"Watch out Repoh, in the corner!" Rue hollered.

Degarne appeared from the shadows in the corner, followed by three massive H.T. combatants. When Degarne noticed Sephora, he was furious.

He remembered her face from the subway. At the time, he had thought she was just another walking soul. Degarne was not used to being duped. He was usually meticulous at his job. Being tricked by Sephora and Repoh really enraged him. Before he could take a step toward Sephora, the troops went at each other. Degarne backed into the dark corner again. Repoh and the girls took cover, behind their troops. As the fight ensued, Sephora checked on Michaela and Rue.

Both were happy to see the extraction team. As big as the Broken soldiers were, they were no match for the C.O.A. troops. When the last of the three Broken soldiers went down, Degarne made a run for it. Sephora told the soldiers to let him go. There was no time to waste chasing Degarne. One of the soldiers bent the bars of the cell with his staff, so that Michaela and Rue could climb through. The other two soldiers carried the injured Broken guards to the cell and stuffed them inside.

Sephora radioed Sergeant Peter, to let him know that they were on the way out. He gave her the all clear. Two warriors led the way out through the vent, while the other two took up the rear. They all took the route that Repoh had taken in. They needed to move fast, before Degarne had a chance to warn Covah and Soahc about the break-in. The back of the building had been secured. The sentries that were told to hold their position on the rooftop were now positioned on the backside of the building, to retrieve the team as they emerged. The troops at the front were told to hit the front door even harder, while the team travelled through the air ducts. General James knew that H.T. would keep the majority of their troops waiting inside, to protect the building.

The troops had already caved in part of the front door, when Repoh and the others reached the outside wall of the air duct, on the backside of the building. The rooftop soldiers led by Sergeant Mathew, met them when they exited. Once they were all safely away from H.T. headquarters, General James gave Sergeant Peter the order to retreat from the H.T. building and meet up with Sergeant Mathew, then make their way back to Pittsburgh, as soon as possible.

The Broken were surprised to see the angels retreat from the building, especially given how close they were to breaking in. Covah and Soahc were given the news about Rue and Michaela's escape, just after the soldiers began fleeing the scene. Covah opened the front door to assess the damages. There were wounded troops sprawled everywhere around the grounds. Soahc had sent people out to gather the wounded and bring them inside. He assigned additional soldiers to round up the deserters. After a quick surveillance outside, Covah returned inside to gather as many men as he could to go after the C.O.A. troops before they left the city. Covah was not looking forward to his next meeting with Lucifer. He could only imagine the C.E.O., as he sat in his office fuming. For the moment, Covah was more concerned with damage control. A Broken agent was in a room with headphones, listening for information from a planted device and taking notes, when it went dead.

One of the angel soldiers had noticed a small light blinking attached to Rue's collar. The soldier picked it off and flung it into the Hudson River as they left the city. He asked Rue if he and Michaela had talked about the location of the safe house. Rue told the soldier that they hadn't, but went over their conversation in his mind.

In Pittsburgh, General James informed everyone in the command center that the troops were on their way home with Rue and Michaela. The ninety-eighth floor was packed with workers. Everyone was ecstatic with the news, but General James reminded them that they were not out of the woods yet. There was still work to be done. Mark and his team kept an eye on the cameras placed outside of H.T. headquarters, so that they could let the general know when H.T.'s posse was on the way. Soldiers from satellite offices joined the troops as they made their way back to Pittsburgh to strengthen the group, just in case there was another confrontation with the Broken.

The battle that had seemed like hours to the Broken had only lasted about forty-five minutes. Covah had finally gotten his people together and they began to leave H.T. headquarters by five-thirty a.m. The sun had just started to rise when they took chase. The extraction militia had already passed by Harrisburg when Covah's soldiers finally got moving. C.O.A. soldiers moved faster and grew stronger as they picked up more warriors, each time they passed another satellite office. By the time Covah and his soldiers caught a glimpse of the angels, they had made it to the outskirts of Pittsburgh. It looked like the C.O.A. soldiers were at least three-hundred strong now. Even if Covah's army had caught up with them, they wouldn't have the manpower to match the C.O.A. opposition. Covah turned his soldiers around and headed back to New York, to face the consequences.

Covah noticed the C.O.A. billboards that had cropped up everywhere. The more he noticed them, the more exasperated he became. Most of them contained the catch phrase: *With indifference everywhere, dare to be different. Believe.* Every time Covah passed one of the billboards, it was like a hot dagger poking him in the gut.

CHAPTER 24

The eight-o'clock meeting in all departments started out as more of a celebration. By then, everyone was well aware of the successful rescue of Michaela and Rue from H.T. headquarters. At that time, the two of them were being debriefed on the ninety-eighth floor, by General James and Mark's Intelligence team, while the events were still fresh in their minds. Even though undercover work would be tough for Sephora and her partners now, she and Serafina were very happy to have their teammate back, safe and sound. The news of Repoh's idea to infiltrate the air ducts had given him accolades, and a newfound respect among the employees of C.O.A.

During the questioning, Rue and Michaela were asked to describe their surroundings. How many guards were stationed on the floor? How were they escorted to the cells? Did anything about the layout of the building come to mind? The intelligence team wanted to update their blueprints for the building, in case they may be needed for the future reference. They were also asked about the bug that had been planted on Rue. Michaela and Rue were both adamant that they had not disclosed the safe house location. Most of their conversation had revolved around keeping Rue calm and escaping. Once they were satisfied with the information received, the team turned their questions to matters at hand.

"While you were being held hostage, did you hear anything that might help with H.T.'s plans concerning Pittsburgh?" Mark asked.

Michaela spoke up, "You know, it's a weird thing. The Broken set up the air ducts in the building so that the cries of the prisoners would resonate throughout the building, but they didn't realize it worked both ways."

Rue broke in, "When the inmates quiet down, you are able to pick up conversations from upstairs also."

That piqued General James' interest, "So what were you able to find out?"

"Once we were able to quiet the noise in the cells, we heard some chatter about the businessman in New York. We were able to catch his first name, Bartholomew. We weren't able to get a last name. We do know that he is in Real Estate," Michaela replied.

Mark piped in, "We can run it through the database. It shouldn't be too hard to find a New York Real Estate mogul with that first name."

"Anything else you can think of?' General James asked.

"We did hear that he is very interested in sports, but not sure what his angle is," Rue added.

"Well, that gives us something to go on for now. Thank you both for your help. If you think of anything else that might help our investigation, please let us know. We're going to let you both get some rest. It's been a tough week for you. We will be in touch later. Thank you for the information. You both have been very helpful," General James said as he opened the office door for Michaela and Rue.

After Rue and Michaela left, General James spoke to Mark, "Let me know as soon as you find Bartholomew's last name."

"I will do that, Sir. I will also try to find out his interests. We have the Pirates, Steelers and Penguins. He must have an interest in one of those teams," Mark responded.

"The way Degarne has been hanging around the river at the Point, I have a feeling that it isn't the Penguins. I don't want to speculate. Let's wait until we know more about the man," General James added.

"Noted," Mark said. "We will get back to you soon."

"Thank you," General James replied on his way out of the room. He needed to check in with his troops that were being held at C.O.A. until further notice.

The Pittsburgh office was almost at full capacity, with the extra military presence of approximately three-hundred troops stationed there. The soldiers from the satellite offices had been sent back to their home posts, since everyone had made it safely back home in Pittsburgh. Rue and Repoh were being put up on the ninety-seventh floor with Sephora, Serafina and Michaela, along with a few guards to keep them safe.

Although it had been a grueling week for Rue, the last thing he planned to do was rest up. He finally had the chance to sit down and have a conversation with his brother, without prying ears listening in. The two of them were happy to be at C.O.A. They felt comfortable and safe there. They had a lot to catch up on. They discussed how they both hated their jobs at H.T., and what they had been forced to do, for the good of the company. They discussed how the only thing they liked about their job was being let outside of H.T. headquarters. The only thing they didn't discuss was what they both had on their minds. What would become of them now? They knew they would never be able to go back to the company. Each of them had decided that would be a topic for another time. For the moment, they just wanted to get to know each other again.

Gabriel and Sarah continued their daily updates with Josh Alexander. The workload had become so overwhelming for Josh that the team talked to their supervisor about getting some compensation for him. The supervisor agreed that it was a good idea. Sarah was able to convince local churches to donate money, to be used for a small salary for Josh. She didn't have much trouble persuading them, once they realized that the work he was doing would encourage people to visit local churches. Josh was pleased to accept the offer. They talked about starting another discussion group just for youths. Josh said that his nephew had expressed interest. Gabriel told Josh that he would speak to friends that could be interested in talking to Boys & Girls Clubs of America, Boy Scouts, Girl Scouts and other organizations. Gabriel and Sarah would post flyers at C.O.A. They were sure that employees would show interest in the idea.

Upon Covah's return, and before he'd had time to catch his breath from chasing after C.O.A., Lucifer called for a meeting in his office. Covah, Degarne, Soahc and a few other managers were in attendance. The C.E.O. wanted answers. How long had Rue and Repoh been working for C.O.A.? Why didn't anyone know about it? How did they know to go through the air vents? The list went on and on. Covah, Degarne, and Soahc took the brunt of the brow beatings, but as everyone knows, excrement rolls downhill. By the end of the day, some prisoners would be released, more would be imprisoned, and many soldiers would be replaced. As always was the case at H.T., someone was waiting to take another's place in a heartbeat. Lucifer wanted the mess cleaned up in a hurry. Once that was taken care of, they would meet again to discuss plans going forward, regarding their latest project. Lucifer also revealed to the leaders that the bug planted on Rue had proved useless. Lucifer belittled Covah for not interrogating the two when he had the chance. Covah knew he would have to make up for his mistakes, and soon.

When Mark had a break in the action, he phoned Thomas at the San Francisco office. He gave him the low down on the activities that had taken place the night before. Mark asked how things were going on his end. Were they still watching Regna? Thomas informed Mark that Regna had indeed been spending time on Camarillo Street, again. Informants had confirmed that Regna was doing business with Jedidiah Compton. In fact, he had funded the upgrades for the old theatre, through H.T. of course.

Jedidiah Compton had no theological training whatsoever. In fact, the only religious background he had was when he was a young child and his mother dragged him to church on holidays. After he had spent time in jail a time or two for swindling people, Jedidiah decided to find another way to make some fast money that wasn't quite as dangerous. He had spent some time watching T.V. preachers and he couldn't believe how many people were willing to just hand over their hard earned money to these people. The best part was that it was legal and tax free. The thing that surprised Jedidiah more than anything was how easy it was to get a license to start his own church. He started out with a small, low rent building in North Hollywood. Before long his church had grown with followers, which was when he met Regna. Jedidiah saw Regna as just another dupe that he could use for his money. He gladly accepted help from Regna to fund the remodeling of his new church. At that time, Jedidiah had no idea who Regna worked for. Construction was about to be finished up, and Jedidiah couldn't wait to fill those collection baskets.

General James met with Sergeants Peter and Mathew, and their men to make sure that all of the soldiers had found a place to rest. He hadn't expected a visit from H.T., but didn't want to be caught off guard either. He told all of them how proud he was, to be in command of such skilled soldiers, and how they had fought bravely and without hesitation. They had accomplished their objective through teamwork and dedication. The soldiers really appreciated hearing those encouraging words from their commanding officer. They knew that the H.T. soldiers would certainly not be hearing the same gratitude coming from their superiors.

After he left the troops, General James returned to the ninety-eighth floor to check in with Mark. Mark's team had found some interesting information on Bartholomew. His last name was Jenkins. He owned several office buildings in New York City. He was a ruthless man that cared more about money than anything else. The only other thing that seemed to interest him was baseball. In his youth, he'd played college ball at Penn State University, but wasn't good enough to make it to the majors. He had made more money than most people could ever dream of in his lifetime, but Bartholomew always regretted the one thing he couldn't have.

CHAPTER 25

By the next morning, Michaela seemed to be back to her old self already. She was complaining about having to work in the office, instead of being in the field.

"Are you nuts?" Serafina exclaimed. "You just got rescued from a jail cell at H.T., and now you want to get back out there? Geeze!"

"I know, but I just hate being cooped up," Michaela complained.

Sephora shook her head and laughed, "There is plenty here to keep us busy, Michaela. Mark needs help compiling information on Bartholomew. The Broken are planning something big, and we will do what we can to stop another disaster from happening, and we will do it with a smile, right?"

"Right." Michaela flashed a fake smile at Sephora, then turned and shot a gagging face at Serafina. Serafina raised an eyebrow and smirked at Michaela, then returned to working on her computer.

Michaela hadn't been the only one tired of being cooped up. Jeremiah noticed that Jonah was becoming restless as well. Jeremiah pulled Jonah out into the hall, to show him Gabriel and Sarah's flyer, which asked for volunteers to talk to young people about starting a discussion group. Jonah read the flyer while his protégé, Theo, looked over his shoulder.

"Let's do it Jonah," Theo spoke up.

"It's right up your alley Jonah," Jeremiah said, encouragingly. "You would be a natural. You're funny, you like kids, and you definitely like to talk."

Jonah rubbed his chin, "You think so newbie?"

"Sure it will be fun," Theo countered.

"Okay, sign us up, Jeremiah," Jonah replied.

Jeremiah was pleased that Jonah said yes. It would keep him and Theo occupied while temporary restrictions were in place, and the team would get outside for a while.

Repoh and Rue had also seen the flyers, and thought it would be a great way to help out. It would give them something to do, and it would also help out C.O.A., at the same time. Rue thought that they would be perfect for the job, since they knew what could happen in a blink of an eye. They were living proof of having made the wrong decision in life. Repoh agreed, then took Gabriel's number off of the flyer and made the call. Gabriel was glad that the two were interested, but needed to talk to his superiors about keeping them safe, outside C.O.A. headquarters. He promised to get back to Repoh on the matter.

The construction workers had all gone, except for one, who just finished checking the sign on the old theatre. Jedidiah stood out front, as the electrician hit the switch that lit up his name. He couldn't have been happier to see his name in lights. Two more days until the big debut. Regna and his people had been spreading out flyers of their own, for the event. If everything went as planned, Jedidiah would be leading a thousand or so people down the wrong path shortly.

Covah and Soahc made sure that the air vents had been reinforced, and workers were re-routing the system to make it impenetrable for any future, unseen infiltrators. Additional guards had been placed at the outside openings, just to be safe. The front door had been repaired and the building looked to be back to normal. All the employees were on edge, knowing that management was not happy with the lot of them at the moment, and the attack had spooked most of them as well.

Degarne met with Covah, Soahc and the C.E.O., to discuss plans for the upcoming Pittsburgh visit. With the air vents repaired, prying ears were unable to listen in on the meeting notes.

Mark and his team were busy scanning through many articles about Bartholomew Jenkins. For someone with so much money, he was not very well liked. He had a reputation for clawing his way to the top, no matter who paid the price. Apparently he hadn't even trusted his closest advisors. It seemed he didn't have many friends. He spent time with a lot of women, but had no long-term relationships, and had no children. If Bartholomew had a good side, it was not evident from any of the research that had been collected on the man. The intelligence team had been trying to get a look at his schedule. At that point, no mention of a visit to Pittsburgh was found. He was currently in his apartment at City Bank-Farmers Trust Building on Exchange Place. Not too far from H.T. headquarters. The City Bank-Farmers Trust Building was the fourth largest building in the world, when it had been constructed in 1931. They were considered to have been the most luxurious apartments in the city, complete with marble floors, custom cabinets and appliances. There was even a sundeck, overlooking the city. The apartment was just one of many homes that Bartholomew owned. It was where he spent most of his time, high above the city. The living room was filled with his trophies, from little league through college, along with a few pictures of Roberto Clemente and Honus Wagner. Former Pittsburgh Pirate legends.

Sephora, Serafina and Michaela had gotten so used to seeing Noah that they kind of missed their daily meetings with him. Michaela thought it was funny how someone could drive you crazy when you are with them, then when they are out of sight, you find yourself thinking about them. Noah seemed to have found it a little boring with the girls gone too. He had gotten back into his normal grind in the office.

Gabriel and Sarah met with their friends at the gym, and found out that one of the couples had a teenage son who was interested in working with the youth discussion group. Gabriel mentioned that he would let Josh Alexander know that evening. The teenager could get together with Josh's nephew and work out a plan. Gabriel's supervisor liked the idea of Repoh and Rue working with the team, but they would need to meet with the community leaders close to C.O.A. headquarters, where they could be protected. He didn't want to take any chances of Degarne or his team coming after the brothers again. Gabriel assured his boss that he and Sarah would work things out with that in mind.

Employees that had been sent on assignments outside of C.O.A. headquarters had been accompanied by soldiers. General James wanted to keep his troops alert, and all of the employees safe. Even though there had been no reports of extraordinary traffic by the Broken, it was just a precaution. Luckily, it was a pretty quiet day for assignments. There were mostly traffic problems and a few emergency situations, but nothing catastrophic.

The project leaders hoped that it would stay that way.

Jeremiah had been amused by Jonah and Theo, who were digging through a box of Boy Scout paraphernalia that the warehouse had dropped off. The two of them had been busy trying on uniforms. Jonah was wearing a pair of scout leader shorts and a shirt that was one size too small. The buttons were about to burst. He applied a sash, with merit badges attached, and a hat to complete the ensemble, before he admired himself in the mirror.

"What do you think Jeremiah?" Jonah asked, as he waited for approval.

"Oh, you're definitely going to make an impression. That's for sure," Jeremiah said, as he covered the smile on his face.

"Are you sure these shorts don't make my rear end look too fat?" Jonah asked as serious as could be.

"I don't think it's the shorts Jonah," Jeremiah replied, trying to hold back his laughter.

Jonah waved Jeremiah off, "Oh, what do you know anyway?"

Jonah continued to look in the mirror, while Theo wiped some lint off of Jonah's back.

Sephora, Serafina and Michaela had been put on surveillance duty. They had relentlessly watched the video feeds around H.T. headquarters. Mark figured it would be a good assignment for them, since they had spent so much time in New York, and were accustomed to the traffic patterns and familiar with the Broken's faces. For a long time, there had been little movement in and out of the building, other than the soldiers relieving one another. Within a few hours, a familiar face had emerged from the building. It was Degarne and he had a few soldiers shadowing him. The girls followed his trail through several cameras. He didn't go too far. The soldiers waited outside, as Degarne entered the City Bank Farmers-Trust Building.

"Gotcha!" Sephora shouted. "Mark, you have to see this!"

"Finally, we can tie him to Bartholomew. Good work ladies!" Mark exclaimed, then he disappeared, to find General James and give him the news.

CHAPTER 26

Two days had passed without incident at C.O.A. Pittsburgh. The girls had worked surveillance non-stop. Degarne had spent an hour inside the City Bank Farmers-Trust Building the other day, but hadn't returned since then. Upon his return from his visit to Bartholomew's apartment building, Degarne had remained inside H.T. headquarters. Michaela had kept close tabs on Bartholomew Jenkins. He'd had a driver pick him up the night before. He had dinner at a restaurant in Manhattan, where he met an unknown female companion. After the meal, Bartholomew returned to his apartment alone and hadn't left the building since then. Mark assigned a few employees to research the Pittsburgh Pirate organization. He wanted to see if there was any correlation between the team and Bartholomew Jenkins. So far, no connection had been found. Mark asked the team to keep digging. The ball club hadn't had a winning season in a very long time, but avid fans had kept their support for the team. The Pirates remained solvent, with no money problems that could tie the real estate mogul to the business. Mark called Noah and asked him to look into Bartholomew as well. Being that he was in New York, Mark thought Noah may be able to find some dirt on the businessman.

Jedidiah Compton had been getting ready for his big night in North Hollywood. The old theatre looked great, with the remodeling finished. He had tested the microphones to make sure that he could be heard throughout the theatre. He had a couple of assistants outfitted with headsets, who had been roaming the building. They talked to Jedidiah as they moved around, while he made sure he could hear them clearly. They would relay pertinent information regarding the guests to Jedidiah, to be used during the performance. Lighting engineers made sure that all the spotlights were operating correctly. Once Jedidiah was satisfied that everything was in working order, he returned to an office to work on his sermon.

Thomas and his west coast team had been watching Regna and Jedidiah. Thomas figured that Regna would be attending Jedidiah's debut. Regna had no idea that Thomas would have some of his people in attendance also. Until now, Regna had only been observed through the cameras. They wanted Regna to continue to think he was incognito.

About twenty minutes before the revival had begun, Jedidiah took a peek between the curtains. The house was seventy-five percent full. Walking souls were talking over the band, which Jedidiah had hired the day before. They were mediocre at best, and didn't know any gospel music to speak of. Jedidiah told them to play whatever jazz tunes that they were familiar with. By then, the main theatre was full, and people were making their way to the balcony. Jedidiah noticed Regna seated front and center. He nodded and smiled. Regna returned the gesture. Jedidiah returned backstage and checked in with his assistants, who were on the other end of the headsets, to make sure they were ready.

With a motion from a stage assistant, the music ceased, then a drum roll prompted Jedidiah's entrance. Spot lights circled the stage momentarily, then centered on Jedidiah. Applause ensued in the theatre, as Jedidiah raised his hands to the crowd and took a bow. He felt like a movie star.

Once the applause had quieted down, Jedidiah began to speak, "God wants you to know that you are special. He wants you to have everything that you desire! Health, wealth and happiness is what He wants for you!" The entire building cheered. Regna was smiling.

Jedidiah gave it a minute, then continued, "There is nothing wrong with wanting more out of life. He wants us to prosper. He wants you to be healthy!" Jedidiah lowered his head and touched his earpiece. "I know that there is someone here tonight with eye problems. Let me see…I am getting a name. First name is Toby. Toby has macular degeneration."

A man stood up in the middle of the theatre and raised his hand, "That's me!"

"Come down here Toby," Jedidiah shouted.

A woman took the man by his arm and led him down the aisle. Jedidiah placed his hand on Toby's eyes and shoved him backwards. Two men caught Toby and laid him on the floor of the stage. Toby sat back up, then was helped to his feet again by the two men. He shouted thank you as the woman helped him back to his seat. Jedidiah continued to call out names of walking souls in the audience, with different types of afflictions, and bring them forward. Once everyone had been enthralled in the moment, it was time to pass the collection basket.

After all of the baskets had been collected, Jedidiah started to preach again. He was on a roll. He had gotten the audience pumped up, and made everything seem rosy. Not once did he mention anything about helping each other, or getting along with one another. Everything had revolved around making yourself feel good. The audience had eaten up every word, especially Regna.

Jedidiah felt pretty self-confident at that point, so he asked if anyone in the audience had anything to share with the audience. Someone in the left hand corner stood up and shouted, "I do."

The spotlight moved in, to shine on the man. It was one of Thomas' employees named Francis. "Tell me, what direction does God want me to take in my life?" he asked.

The spot light turned and shined directly in Jedidiah's eyes; he held his hand up to shade the light so he could see the man's face. Francis had changed his appearance so that Jedidiah could see his wings. Jedidiah rubbed his eyes, he thought that he was seeing things. When he opened his eyes again he still saw the man with wings. With Jedidiah speechless, all heads turned to see Francis. Everyone wondered what was wrong with Jedidiah. All they saw was an ordinary looking man. Everyone but Jedidiah and Regna. Regna stood up and leaned toward Jedidiah, and said, "Get it together. You're going to ruin everything!"

Jedidiah had broken into a cold sweat, but tried to regain his composure, "Um, God wants you to follow your dream."

Before Jedidiah had time to catch his breath, another angel stood up, wings and all.

The angel asked, "Is it wrong for me to cut benefits for my employees, even though we've made record profits this year?"

Jedidiah's legs had gotten wobbly, so he reached for the stool next to him on the stage, to sit down. People whispered to each other as they watched Jedidiah fall apart on the stage. Again Jedidiah tried to recover his self-control, then responded, "You may want to rethink that decision, my friend."

At that point, the angels gave Jedidiah complete sight of the angels and Broken in the auditorium. He saw the red eyes of the Broken throughout the theatre. Then he saw Regna in his true state. The sight of Regna frightened Jedidiah so bad that he fell backwards off his stool and landed flat on his back. Jedidiah jumped up and ran screaming from the stage. As the audience stood to see what had happened, Regna and his entourage stood, then quickly and quietly left the theatre. Regna was furious that he had been blindsided. Another plan had been ruined at the hand of C.O.A., and Lucifer would not be happy to receive that news.

In his haste, Jedidiah hadn't stopped to pick up his jacket on the way out, let alone all of the cash that he had left behind in the collection baskets. He jumped into his car and hightailed it out of town. He wanted to get as far away from Hollywood as possible. He thought that somewhere on the east coast would be a good place to move to. He would have plenty of time to try and understand what had just happened, during his drive. It would be a little while before Jedidiah realized that he would be lucky if he had enough cash in his pocket to make it to Bakersfield.

The people in the auditorium waited for a few minutes, just to see if Jedidiah had planned on coming back. At first they thought it could be part of his performance. The guests hadn't seen what Jedidiah had just witnessed, and neither did his assistants. Once the walking souls figured out that he had no intention of returning, they filed out of the theatre bewildered. Once the band and other employees of Jedidiah noticed that his car was gone, they left the building as well.

After a few hours, Jedidiah Compton had stopped for gas in a little California town called Mentone. That was when he realized that he had only three-hundred fifty dollars to his name. He had still been reeling from the events that had taken place. He had no plans to return to Hollywood, no matter how much money he had left behind. While he was pumping gas, he noticed a help wanted sign at a diner next door. Across the street, there was a fleabag motel. Jedidiah figured he probably had enough cash to afford a week's rent at the hotel. He finished pumping gas, then went next door to get something to eat and apply for the dishwasher job at the diner. It was a far different situation from where he was a few hours earlier, but he thought maybe it was time to make an honest living for a change.

The angels that had turned Jedidiah's world upside down, had returned the donations to many of the walking souls on their way out. They also paid the band, but not the assistants, who had helped Jedidiah dupe the people in the audience. What was left was donated to a local shelter. The deed to the theatre would be given to a hard working pastor in the community that had been preaching out of a rundown building for years, just in case Jedidiah had any ideas of returning.

CHAPTER 27

Gabriel and Sarah had set up a meeting for Jonah, with the Boy Scouts. Of course, he wore his scout uniform to the meeting, against Jeremiah's protest. The meeting actually went well. Jonah was funny and charming, and they were impressed with the idea. The leaders promised to propose the idea of a youth discussion group with all of the troops in the area. They would get back to Jonah with names of kids that expressed interest in the project. They told Jonah that they had seen all of the billboards in the area, and how many of the kids really liked the slogan. Jonah was happy to hear that the message had reached the young people.

Gabriel and Sarah were trying to have the Boys & Girls Club leaders come into the city, so that Repoh and Rue wouldn't have to stray too far from headquarters. Once the execs had a chance to check their schedules, they would get back to the team. Rue and Repoh looked forward to helping out in some way. Even though they had helped C.O.A. immensely, the two of them had not been invited into the intelligence room. The brothers were getting bored with sitting around. Gabriel told them that if things didn't work out with the project, he would talk to his boss to find something in customer service for the two of them to occupy their time.

Thomas had talked to Mark earlier in the morning and described the whole Jedidiah ordeal. Mark passed on the story, and the employees were excited about the two victories that the corporation had experienced in one week. They wouldn't dwell on their triumphs, since they knew the Broken had something up their sleeve. Sephora and Serafina were watching for Degarne, but he was still hunkered down at H.T. headquarters. Michaela had found out that Bartholomew Jenkins booked a flight to Pittsburgh, for the following morning. With Bartholomew scheduled to come to the city, the team knew that Degarne would not be far behind.

The employees that Mark had assigned to look into the Pirates, checked the schedule for upcoming games. It turned out that the Yankees were coming to town for ball games the very next day and the following evening. Mark immediately contacted General James for an emergency meeting with some of the staff. Sergeants Peter and Mathew were invited along with Sephora, Serafina and Michaela. Once everyone was in attendance, General James stood and began to speak, "Given the circumstances, I've ordered more troops here to the city from of our satellite offices. They will be arriving here shortly. With the Yankees in town, we expect attendance at PNC Park to be sold out for both games. We anticipate that Degarne will be making his way to Pittsburgh before long. Mark, what would you like to say?"

Mark responded, "Thanks General. Along with a military presence at both games, we want to place additional people in security positions. We will be using some of our customer service reps in that regard. The customer service supervisor will be in charge of assigning those positions." Mark motioned to the supervisor seated next to him. The supervisor nodded, but remained quiet.

Again, General James took the reins, "We will send the same platoons that were used in New York, to PNC Park. We will keep a low profile outside the park. We don't want the Broken to realize they are under surveillance. If need be, the rest of our army can be here dispatched from headquarters. Sephora and Serafina will keep us apprised of Degarne's whereabouts. Michaela will be watching Bartholomew Jenkins. We don't foresee any trouble at the day game tomorrow. We are most concerned with the night game that is scheduled for the following evening. Unless you have anything to add Mark, that's all for now."

"I think we've covered everything for the time being, General," Mark replied.

"Then we can adjourn for now. Let's get back to work then," General James concluded.

The command center was full. Employees that weren't watching video feeds were busy researching information pertinent to the case. One of the staff had found an article that mentioned Bartholomew's company, from two years ago. It was short, but stated the company's interest in purchasing a baseball team. The article revealed two teams in particular. One was the Chicago Cubs, and the other was the Pittsburgh Pirates. When a spokesman for the company was asked to comment, he said that it was unsubstantiated speculation. There were no further articles that tied Bartholomew to the team, but Mark thought one was enough cause for concern. He would alert General James of the new information.

The customer service supervisor had made his decision on security for the Pirate game. Gabriel and Sarah would cover two sections in the outfield. Jeremiah, Jonah and Theo would work near the main entrance of the park. Sephora and her team would monitor the game from the command center. Repoh had pleaded with Sephora to talk Mark into letting him and Rue take part in the security detail. She told him that it was too risky, but she could possibly convince Mark to let the two of them watch the cameras, during the game. Maybe they could help identify some of the Broken in the crowd of fans. Repoh accepted the consolation offer for the moment.

Jonah was thrilled to be picked for the security detail. The two hobbies that Jonah enjoyed most were riding motorcycles and watching sports, especially Pittsburgh teams. He had already looked through the box of clothes for a baseball hat. He stopped briefly and asked Jeremiah, "Do you think I could take a glove with me to the game?"

"No, Jonah. We will be working. You won't have time to catch foul balls!" Jeremiah scolded Jonah, as Theo let out a snort in the background. Jonah ignored Jeremiah and continued to root through his box of clothing.

H.T. headquarters was still sealed up tight, with guards patrolling the perimeter. There had been a lot of chatter among the employees, regarding Repoh and Rue. Most of the gossip revolved around what the consequences would be when they were caught. That idle talk enraged Degarne, because it reminded him that he had failed, which didn't sit well with him or his boss. He knew that the next mission needed to be a success. He was given a pass last time, due to his accomplishments in the past, but he knew it wouldn't happen again. The employees muttered among themselves, as they contemplated what the next step would be. No one had any ideas. There were sporadic meetings throughout the day between Lucifer, Covah, Soahc and Degarne only. None of the other managers had been invited.

Due to concerns of loose lips, the employees would be informed of their participation only when it was required.

Gabriel and Sarah had met with Josh Alexander to inform him that they would be busy for the next few days. Josh seemed to be fine with the news. He appeared to be handling his new position with ease. He had been more comfortable speaking to crowds, and the people seemed to like his leadership qualities. Sarah assured Josh that they would only be a phone call away. Josh assured the team that everything was going great, and that she and Gabriel didn't have to worry. He would be fine. The two of them promised to see him in a few days before they left. They needed to return to headquarters for further instructions and get ready for the next day's events.

That evening, there was another consultation in the command center, to go over the information for the next day. Mark assigned two agents to shadow Bartholomew after his plane touched down in the city. Two more would follow Degarne, whenever he showed up. The security detail had been all worked out. The soldiers would blend in as much as possible, somewhere in the background of PNC Park. Extra employees were called in to handle surveillance in the command center as needed. After having gone over the plan several times, all that was left was to wait and see what happened.

CHAPTER 28

The next morning, Bartholomew Jenkins' private plane landed at Pittsburgh International Airport at ten a.m. A car had been waiting for him when he arrived alone. The driver took him to Hotel Monaco in the heart of the city. It was an upscale hotel, with all of the amenities that catered to people with money. Hotel Monaco was within minutes from PNC Park, and not far from C.O.A. headquarters. The surveillance team waited outside the building as Bartholomew checked in, and then adjourned to his suite. Michaela also had eyes on the hotel from the monitor in the office.

Sephora and Serafina were diligently scanning the footage of the H.T. building for signs of Degarne, when he had left the structure. There were no sign of him yet. H.T. headquarters was still surrounded with sentries. There was not much traffic that had moved in or out of the building during the morning. General James and Mark had another briefing, to make sure all plans were in place. Soldiers would be dispatched shortly, in small groups, so as not to alert the Broken. They were not to enter the ball park unless notified by their commanding officer. They would be posted all around the perimeter of PNC Park. Repoh and Rue had been invited to the command center once the consultation was finished.

It was a brisk spring morning, but it was expected to warm up into the fifties for the 1:05 p.m. game. By eleven o'clock most of the armed forces had streamed out of the C.O.A. building, to their posts. The security detail would enter the ball park by eleven-thirty. Jeremiah and the others would scour the area for abnormalities, before taking their assigned posts.

At noon, Bartholomew met a woman in the lobby of his hotel. She was different from the one that he had met for dinner in New York. She was dressed in casual clothing, as was Bartholomew. He wore a golf shirt and khakis along with a Pirate ball cap. A driver opened the door for the two, and they made their way to the ball park.

Jeremiah worked at the gate entrance. He took the tickets from Bartholomew and his date, returned the stubs, smiled and told the couple to enjoy the game. Jeremiah was surprised to find that Bartholomew wasn't seated in a luxury suite at the ball park. His tickets were box seats, right behind home plate. Jeremiah radioed Jonah, Theo, Gabriel and Sarah that Mr. Jenkins and his date had entered the park. Jonah and Theo were stationed near the escalators, a short walk up the steps from Bartholomew's seats. Jonah had eyes on him, and tapped Theo's arm and moved his eyes in Bartholomew's direction. The target and his companion proceeded directly to their seats, then ordered a hot dog and Iron City beer from one of the vendors.

General James and Mark pestered the girls relentlessly for information about Degarne's whereabouts. Sephora and Serafina assured them that if he had left the building, they would've known it.

After having announced the lineup for the game, a local singer sang the Star Spangled Banner, then the game was underway. There were a surprising amount of New York fans in attendance, and they cheered as the Yankees leadoff batter walked to the plate. Michaela panned the ball park for unusual activity, as Repoh and Rue looked over her shoulder. Neither Repoh nor Rue recognized Bartholomew's date. She was most likely just another walking soul that Bartholomew spent time with, whenever he was in town. There were plenty of Broken in the crowd, but none that Repoh categorized as important, or tied to Degarne in any way. They were probably just employees that had been assigned to the area.

After everyone had been ushered through the gates, Jeremiah joined Jonah and Theo inside the ball park. They continued to scan the area, from first to third base. Gabriel and Sarah climbed up and down, through the various sections of the outfield seats. The all clear had been reported by each of the security detail. Mark advised them to keep looking and to remain sharp. Mark's comment had been mainly to appease General James' anxiety.

Mark knew that his people were on the ball. The soldiers had declared normal conditions outside of the ball park as well.

Noah called in to report to Mark that he and his team had been monitoring H.T. headquarters. Mark put Noah on the speakerphone. He had substantiated Sephora's claim that Degarne had not left the building in New York, and there had been no suspicious movement in the area. He said hello to the girls before he hung up. They were glad to hear his voice, and that he had confirmed what the girls already knew.

By the seventh inning stretch, it had become pretty clear that Degarne had no intention of attending the first game. The Yankees were leading the Pirates 7-2. Some of the fair weather fans had already exited the park. The diehards still held out hope for a comeback win. Bartholomew seemed to have been enjoying the game, but his lady friend appeared to be restless. The angel security teams had been told to keep guard throughout the end of the game. The Pirates tried to rally in the ninth inning with a single by Andrew McCutchen and Neil Walker, then a homerun by Pedro Alvarez which made it 7-5. The next two batters grounded out, before the Pirate's pitcher struck out, which ended the game.

The fans filed out of the ball park somewhat disappointed, but seemed happy that they had seen a Yankee game. Some would return the next day, and hoped for a better outcome for Pittsburgh supporters. After the game, Bartholomew returned to his hotel and had dinner and drinks at the restaurant, before he and his date retired to his room for the evening. C.O.A. guards were posted outside the building during the night.

After the security detail had performed another exhaustive search of PNC Park, they were sent back to headquarters. Most of the military had also been relieved from their posts, and ordered to return to headquarters. A handful would remain in the area for the night. Jonah was content that he had seen what little he did of the ball game, and looked forward to attending the game the following day. The smell of popcorn and hot dogs along with the roar of the crowd had brought back fond memories for him. Jonah spent most of that evening talking about sports with Theo, which allowed Jeremiah some well-deserved quiet time for a change.

The girls, along with Repoh and Rue, kept watch on PNC Park, the H.T. building, and the hotel during the evening. Bartholomew's companion left the hotel by taxi around two a.m. Bartholomew remained in his room when she left. The driver dropped her off at her home in a well-to-do section on the outskirts of town.

During the night, small groups of two and three employees had begun to leave H.T. headquarters. Additional teams had been added to the surveillance monitors. It was hard for the girls to keep up surveillance on everyone, with only Repoh and Rue at hand. The departures were sporadic, but always at least two or more exited at one time. Degarne had not been among the exodus so far. General James was notified and he dispatched more guards to join the forces near PNC Park and Point State Park as well. He expected to receive an account the moment that the army saw any sign of the Broken.

CHAPTER 29

The Broken had continued to leave H.T. headquarters in small groups throughout the morning and early afternoon. Intelligence advised that they were indeed headed into Pennsylvania, towards Pittsburgh. Finally, at approximately three o'clock in the afternoon, Degarne had been spotted leaving the building in New York. He was with an entourage, which included Covah. Repoh and Rue had recognized some of Degarne's crew in tow. Some of which had spied on the two of them in the past.

Bartholomew Jenkins hadn't left the hotel all day. Room service brought him breakfast. After his meal, he had spent some time in the gym, then returned to his suite. Bartholomew had received no phone calls or visitors yet.

General James increased the soldiers around the vicinity of PNC Park. His sergeants in the field hadn't spotted large numbers of Broken in the area. If they were in town, they had to have been in hiding somewhere.

Bartholomew's driver picked him up from the Hotel Monaco promptly at six o'clock. He drove straight to the ball park. The game was to start at 7:05 p.m. Again Jeremiah took Bartholomew's ticket and returned the stub. At that time, Bartholomew was attending the game by himself. Jeremiah radioed Gabriel and Sarah to keep an eye out for Mr. Jenkins. For that game, Bartholomew had a reserved seat in right field. That seemed odd for everyone involved. Why the outfield?

Much to Jeremiah's surprise, Seil had decided to attend the game as well, with Tim Rice. Seil hadn't paid attention to Jeremiah when he took his ticket. As Jeremiah handed the stub back to Seil, he said, "Nice mustache!"

Seil had been caught off guard. He took the stub from Jeremiah, without a word. Seil touched his upper lip and moved on, remembering what happened the last time they had met. Seil and Tim had seats in peanut heaven in right field. Luckily, he hadn't seen Jonah on the way to their seats.

Right before the game had been scheduled to start, Tim Debacco's voice came over the P.A. system and he began to speak, "The Pittsburgh Pirates would like to welcome everyone to Senior Citizen night, here at PNC Park on this brisk spring night." Jeremiah, Jonah and the others looked around the ball park. It was a sea of grey. Debacco continued, "We all hope the weather will hold out for a great game with the New York Yankees!" The crowd began cheering and whistling. The sky was overcast. It had gotten chilly as the sun disappeared behind the clouds.

Gabriel and Sarah kept eyes on Bartholomew, while he watched the game. Gerrit Cole was on the mound for the Pirates. In the first inning, Cole struck out two, then a ground out by McCann stranded one Yankee on base. The Pirates took a 2-0 lead in the bottom of the 1st inning, when Starling Marte hit a double down the right field line. Runners on 1st and 2nd base easily scored, and the fans were thrilled. The Pirates had held the Yankees scoreless through the third inning.

Degarne and Covah had been tracked the whole way to Pittsburgh. The security detail had been notified that they were in town. General James told the troops to hold their positions. Others could be lurking around the city. The general wanted to wait to see what the H.T. leaders were up to. Rain clouds had moved in fast, and it had begun to sprinkle. In the top of the 6th inning, with two outs, Chase Headley hit a solo home run to make it 2-1, Pirates. Gerrit Cole struck out the next batter, which retired the sides.

Rue had spotted Covah on the monitor; he had entered the ball park. He was seen on the third base side. Theo saw him standing outside of section 109, near a concession stand, and alerted Jonah and Jeremiah. It was a high traffic area. Jeremiah advised Jonah to hold his position near the escalators, and watch for Degarne. Jeremiah would join Theo on that side of the park. Covah jumped around the sections, which kept Jeremiah and Theo on their toes.

Just as the Pirates had stranded two runners on base to end the 6th inning, it began to pour. Tim Debacco announced a rain delay over the system, then the grounds crew hurriedly rolled tarps out onto the field. Fans ran for shelter from the rain. It was a good time for fans to use the bathroom, and get something to eat or drink. With the crowds huddled together, it made it harder for the angels to locate Degarne.

Jonah was overwhelmed with the crowds of people. He found a bench next to the escalator that he could stand on to see over the hordes of walking souls. Within seconds, Jonah saw a figure emerge from the men's room who had tried his best to cover his face. It was Degarne, and he was moving fast. Jonah hollered out Degarne's name. He turned long enough for Jonah to identify his face, then he was gone. Jonah radioed the others, then pushed his way through the line at the bathroom. Jonah screamed at everyone to leave the bathroom. Amid protests, the men retreated, mainly due to the crazed look on Jonah's face. As Jonah searched the last stall, he found what he had feared. It was a homemade bomb. Jonah moved as fast as possible, pushing walking souls out of his way. He radioed for backup as he rushed to the closest exit of PNC Park.

Bartholomew Jenkins never left his right field seat. He sat patiently in the rain as he held an umbrella over his head. General James deployed more troops to the park, and ordered the soldiers to move in quickly. Throughout all the excitement, Sephora was the first one to notice that Repoh and Rue had disappeared from the command center.

Jonah made his way toward the river with the bomb. The Broken came from all sides as he dodged his way past them, towards the water. They had been hiding along the river on both sides. When Jonah was nearly thirty feet from shore, he was tackled by a swarm of Broken. He flung the bomb as hard as he could, in the direction of the river. It exploded right before hitting the water. The blast took out ten of the Broken's army at the shoreline. Jonah was no competition for the twenty soldiers that had him pinned down on the ground. His beating ceased, and when he looked to see why, a group of C.O.A. militia scooped him up and carried him to safety.

Most of the fans that had waited out the rain delay thought that they heard thunder when the bomb blew. A group of older people and some small children were now gathered near the outfield fence. They were gazing toward the river. Large groups of the Broken army had moved in, from the opposite side of the water. Red eyes reflected off of the water. C.O.A. troops met them halfway. Walking souls cheered as the two armies clashed with a thunderous boom, which was heard only by the older sick and the very young. Remember, it was senior citizen day at PNC, and what a show they were getting. As the onlookers grew, many people tried to see what the commotion was all about. Of course they didn't understand the attraction.

Repoh and Rue had followed the last of the soldiers deployed to PNC Park, and joined in the battle, right along with the C.O.A. army. Covah led his troops during the skirmish. C.O.A.'s war cry was almost deafening, but the walking souls cheered on just the same. With their staffs in hand, they shoved the Broken to the other side of the river. Degarne's rage overcame him, when he noticed Repoh and Rue. He headed straight for the brothers without hesitation. The years of torture that the brothers had endured at Degarne's hand gave them strength that they didn't know they had. They gave Degarne a beating that he would never forget. The troops that had been assigned to keep watch on the two brothers moved in and finished Degarne off.

With H.T. casualties strewn everywhere, the Broken had been pushed back further into the city. Covah had lost more than half of his soldiers, and C.O.A. reinforcements were coming out of the woodwork. Covah decided that he'd had enough. Against his better judgement, Covah gave the Broken troops the order to retreat. The C.O.A. army kept on their tails until they were far away from the city. The wounded would be left to their own devices.

The rain had subsided by the end of the confrontation. The crowd had grown in the outfield seats. PNC security was called to investigate. When they arrived, the guards could see nothing of interest outside the ball park. Most of the onlookers who witnessed the skirmish chatted about the ordeal as they returned to their seats. With all of the action, Bartholomew had snuck out of the ball park.

The grounds crew removed the tarps from the field to resume the game. Before the players took the field, the Jumbotron started to flash a familiar slogan: *With indifference everywhere, dare to be different. Believe.* A number of walking souls stood and applauded. Especially the people that had observed the clash between C.O.A. and H.T. Enterprises. Some walking souls had thought the message was meant for fans to have faith in their team.

Seil had watched the battle quietly, not wanting Tim Rice to be the wiser. When he saw the slogan flash on the screen, he angrily hollered out, "I'll be damned!" and accidently spilled his beer.

"What's wrong?" Tim asked.

"Nothing, it's fine," Seil responded, as he tried to regain his composure.

Gabriel smiled as the slogan flashed across the screen. He whispered to Sarah, "Way to go Josh!" Josh Alexander had a friend in the organization that had given him a discount to flash the message. It just so happened that it was perfect timing. The team knew at that moment that they had picked the right man for the job.

The Pirates had scored again in the eighth inning with an RBI by McCutchen, and went on to win the game 3-1. Gerrit Cole pitched a great game, giving up only three hits. For many walking souls it would be a night to remember, but for some, it would have nothing to do with the game.

Jonah had been taken back to C.O.A. headquarters along with others, to recuperate from injuries suffered during the battle. Jonah was sore, but he was in good spirits, given the circumstances. He had been soaking up the attention. The news had travelled throughout the corporation by the time he was brought into the infirmary. His teammates, although proud of their friend, let Jonah have his moment in the spotlight.

Housekeeping employees at PNC Park cleaned up the mess left behind by fans. Luckily, it was mostly empty beer cups and such. When the workers turned out the lights in the ball park, most of them had no idea what had really taken place that night. Some of the walking souls that had witnessed the battle kept it to themselves. Others tried to share their experience with family members who had been there. Many of them listened, but nobody could come up with an explanation for the mass hysteria. There were a few that listened, then remembered the slogan that had flashed on the Jumbotron and thought, "Maybe they weren't crazy after all."

General James had kept some troops stationed at the Point for the night. The majority of them had returned to the conference room at C.O.A. He commended the soldiers for a job well done. He applauded his officers for delegating orders, which resulted in a remarkable show of force against the enemy. General James told the men to take advantage of some down time while they could. Some of the soldiers would have to relieve the troops still protecting the city before long.

CHAPTER 30

The next day, H.T. Enterprises had a whole new management team on the east coast, which came as no surprise. Covah and Degarne had finally found out what it felt like to be on the other side of a cell. Of course, the leaders had been spared no sympathy with their fellow inmates. Soahc was imprisoned along with the other two, even though he hadn't taken part in the debacle in Pittsburgh. Lucifer decided it was time for a major change. He had no problem finding eager replacements, who immediately stepped up and took their high ranking positions. Although Mehyam hadn't received word of changes being made on the west coast yet, he was understandably nervous.

The intelligence team had gathered more information regarding Bartholomew Jenkins. It turned out that he had worked out a deal with Degarne. Mr. Jenkins had wanted to buy a professional ball team. He never got over the fact that he didn't make it to the majors, so the next best thing would be to buy a team. The Pirates were not interested in selling. Given the team's record in the last several years, Bartholomew thought through some encouragement, he could get the team for a steal. Degarne came up with the idea of placing the bomb. If the plan had worked, several people would've been hurt and most probably killed. The bathroom where the bomb had been strategically placed was near loadbearing beams. It wasn't strong enough to bring the structure down, but would've been enough to cause some major damage. Bartholomew thought it would deter attendance and waver the owner's tenacity. With the Pirates making the playoffs during the previous year, he wanted it done before they continued another possible winning season.

Jonah felt much better as he joked around with some of the other soldiers in the infirmary, then Sergeant Mathew walked in with two soldiers. They approached Jonah with an official look on their faces. Sergeant Mathew announced, "Jonah, I need you to follow me to A.R."

Jonah looked a little nervous, but replied, "What is this all about?"

"That's above my paygrade. Please follow us," Sergeant Mathew responded.

Jonah followed the soldiers quietly to the ninety-ninth floor. The soldiers had passed the Angel Resources office, which mystified Jonah, then opened the door to the auditorium. Before Jonah could open his mouth, he noticed the auditorium was full of cheering employees. The soldiers led Jonah to a seat on the stage beside Repoh and Rue, who looked as perplexed as Jonah. Jonah noticed Jeremiah and Theo seated in the front row of the audience, which made him feel a little better.

Once the crowd quieted down, Mark stood at the podium and gave thanks to all supervisors and their departments. He mentioned that without teamwork from all employees, things could've turned out completely different. General James took the floor next, and again expressed gratitude to the army. Applause followed each of the speakers. After both had finished speaking, the A.R. Director stepped up to the podium and announced, "Here is someone that needs no introduction."

A figure had been standing off to one side of the altar, out of the limelight. However, the employees couldn't help but notice Him. There was a glow about Him. He had no wings. He was barefoot, and dressed in a pure white robe. The crowd started whispering among themselves, "Jesus... It's Jesus..."

Jesus walked modestly up to the altar. He wanted the employees to be the focus of the assembly on that day. Even so, everyone dropped to their knees in His presence. You could see the love that His employees had for Him. Jesus raised a hand to quiet the crowd.

Jesus approached Repoh and Rue first. He placed a hand on both of their heads, then spoke: "I have seen the loyalty you both have shown to C.O.A. I also see the love in your hearts. Repoh and Rue, you are to remain with us as part of our family now."

The brothers were overcome with joy. They thanked Jesus profusely as they wept and hugged each other. It was the outcome they both had hoped for. Sephora, Serafina and Michaela couldn't have been happier for the brothers.

Jesus then turned His attention to Jonah, "Jonah, you have been called here to acknowledge your part in last night's events."

Jonah looked to Jesus with a worried expression and without a thought, blurted out, "Jesus, I had nothing to do with the outcome of that game!"

"I know you didn't Jonah," Jesus replied.

"Of course, You know. Why wouldn't You?" Jonah responded timidly, as laughter filled the auditorium.

Jesus smiled, touched Jonah's cheek, and replied, "You did good Jonah."

"Thank you Lord," Jonah blushed.

Jeremiah smiled and nodded to Jonah in admiration for his friend and partner.

The End?

For eons, the never-ending struggle of the Broken had been the ultimate act of hopelessness and despair. No matter how hard they tried, they knew deep in their souls that they would never be successful in defeating God's Corporation of Angels. The best that they could hope for was to grab hold of as many walking souls as possible, by enticing them with false expectations to cultivate their cause. As the old saying goes, misery loves company!

Printed in the United States
By Bookmasters